SPECIAL MESSAGE TO READERS

This book is published by

THE ULVERSCROFT FOUNDATION,

a registered charity in the U.K., No. 264873

The Foundation was established in 1974 to provide funds to help towards research, diagnosis and treatment of eye diseases. Below are a few examples of contributions made by THE ULVERSCROFT FOUNDATION:

★ A new Children's Assessment Unit at Moorfield's Hospital, London.

★ Twin operating theatres at the Western Ophthalmic Hospital, London.

★ The Frederick Thorpe Ulverscroft Chair of Ophthalmology at the University of Leicester.

★ Eye Laser equipment to various eye hospitals.

If you would like to help further the work of the Foundation by making a donation or leaving a legacy, every contribution, no matter how small, is received with gratitude. Please write for details to:

THE ULVERSCROFT FOUNDATION,
The Green, Bradgate Road, Anstey,
Leicestershire, LE7 7FU. England.
Telephone: (0533) 364325

Love is
a time of enchantment:
in it all days are fair and all fields
green. Youth is blest by it,
old age made benign: the eyes of love see
roses blooming in December,
and sunshine through rain. Verily
is the time of true-love
a time of enchantment—and
Oh! how eager is woman
to be bewitched!

ONE ENCHANTED SUMMER

At her aunt's request, Tracy Allen left Oregon to work in her bookstore in San Francisco. In the Book Nook Tracy would have considered herself a success had it not been for the unexplained hostility of the manager toward her, and her strong suspicions that something peculiar was going on in the rare book department. A tale of mystery and romance and a girl who found both during one enchanted summer.

ANNE TEDLOOK BROOKS

ONE ENCHANTED SUMMER

Complete and Unabridged

ULVERSCROFT
Leicester

First published in the USA in 1958 by
Arcadia House

First Large Print Edition
published September 1990

British Library CIP Data

Brooks, Anne Tedlook
One enchanted summer.—Large print ed.—
Ulverscroft large print series: romance
I. Title
813′.54[F]

ISBN 0-7089-2277-5

Published by
F. A. Thorpe (Publishing) Ltd.
Anstey, Leicestershire
Set by Rowland Phototypesetting Ltd.
Bury St. Edmunds, Suffolk
Printed and bound in Great Britain by
T. J. Press (Padstow) Ltd., Padstow, Cornwall

1

THE Allen house stood well back from the street. It was a red brick house of two stories and an afterthought of two additions: a family room of generous proportions; and an ell at the rear to house guests. Architecturally speaking, it could easily offend a purist's eyes, but taken as a whole, it had an arresting charm which caused many motorists on a Sunday afternoon to slow at the corner of Linden and Sacajawea to admire it.

On a balmy Sunday afternoon two weeks after Commencement, Tracy Allen sat reading the *Oregonian*. The white benches, the redwood patio furniture and the bright umbrella which she avoided, the better to tan her golden skin, fitted snugly into the picture.

She folded the feature section and placed it neatly on the stack of magazines. Then, leaning back against the trunk of a tree, she began to plan.

Her sisters, Susan and Leslie, were

washing the the station wagon just beyond the service fence. Their voices rose and fell to the sound of running water. Their brother Tom had gone to a picnic today at Silver Creek Falls, and their parents were drowsing over a television program.

The chimes rang and the musical notes reached Tracy's ears in the lull of car washing. She wondered idly who might be ringing the bell. Probably one of the neighbors. She could picture her mother picking up her father's papers, which he still nonchalantly dropped one by one after he perused them. Dad would probably not have heard the bell.

Tracy thought peacefully, It's nice not to have to go to class. It's wonderful to be all through. Yet she had a feeling of emptiness at times when she realized that school did give one a sense of security. You didn't worry about how to spend your time. You *knew*. But now the lethargy of a warm valley summer with its endless hours stretched invitingly before her.

You could get a job, you could do the social rounds of her set, and of course she had Bob Follett.

Bob would be back tonight for another

week. He would be in summer session, after spending a week with his parents in Seattle. It was strange that she had found an odd sort of peace the past few days during Bob's absence. It had been wonderful to curl up in the evening and watch television. She'd even fallen asleep once or twice before the program ended.

"She's exhausted from all the Commencement activities," her mother had said last night.

"I'm just lazy," she'd protested. But there was a kind of saturation point, she supposed. Swimming had helped ease the fatigue in her bones, but that was a different kind of fatigue.

"Tracy!" Her mother's call preceded her plump figure. "Oh, there you are. A letter for you. Don't get excited; it's not from Bob. Aunt Ellen."

Why would Aunt Ellen be wanting to write her? Tracy rose and went to meet her mother.

"I wonder. Ellen's never very good about writing. I do wish she'd leave San Francisco, but she never will."

"Just about as apt to as the Golden Gate," agreed Tracy. She accepted the

3

pale blue envelope which she'd recognized for years as Aunt Ellen's own particular stationery. Not only air mail but also special delivery.

"If you don't mind, I'll wait until you read it. Dad's snoozing away, which is a perfect insult to the program."

"Dear Little Tracy," her niece began to read Ellen Taylor's dainty script: "It's difficult to imagine your being all grown up and graduated at last from the University. I'm hoping, dear, that your own plans are not all set for the summer, or for longer even. I've thought of the most fantastic idea."

Tracy's eyes twinkled. Aunt Ellen's fantastic idea would undoubtedly seem very tame. "Dear, it would be so wonderful if you'd come down and work in our beautiful shop. After all your literature courses and library science, and with your intelligence, it would be an excellent opportunity for you to learn the trade."

Tracy paused numbly. She could see the bookshop, beloved through the years. It was down a little lane, which led away from the busy street and opened on a small court with a garden and a fountain. The

4

bookshop had an intriguing doorway, and a balcony inside. Picturesque, immaculate, it had become famous with the old, wealthy San Franciscans.

Yet for the past few years newer books, best sellers, were finding more and more buyers. Why, Uncle Stanley had even served tea every winter afternoon at three o'clock, and his appreciative clientele flocked in to hear current authors lecture on their books, or sign their names to leather-bound volumes suitable for the customers' shelves.

Tracy stood holding the letter, silently remembering.

"Is it something important?" her mother's voice brought her back.

"Aunt Ellen wants me to come down and work in the Book Nook."

Mrs. Allen was silent for a long moment. Then she asked, "Soon?"

Tracy scanned the rest of the letter. She nodded.

"Oh, dear! just when I thought you would be having a good rest. There's so much to do here, too. And you could run over to the school any time."

"She thinks I might like a career. She offers me a good salary!"

"But your plans!"

"I know. My plans are still in the making. I do love San Francisco, of course. I've never really seen it, except for a quick dash through a museum here and a park there."

"But you'd be so tied down."

"Not really. At least not at first. She says I could work into it gradually: take about six hours a day four days a week, and have some time off for shopping and relaxing, especially the first month or so. She's been going down herself the past month. Listen, Mother. 'Mr. Kennedy let Marcia go last month and has a new man in to take her place. While I trust Blair Kennedy implicitly, I like to know what's being read, and Marcia was a dear to come to tea with me at least once a week. Now that's all changed. I've seen Miles Stewart only three times because he's always so busy. I'm sure my husband knew what he was doing when he hired Mr. Kennedy; still I like to have a little closer connection. The truth, dear, is that sales have fallen off terribly, in spite of additional advertising.

6

With your clever business sense—" Tracy smiled. "Business sense!"

"Sounds to me as though Ellen is worried. Dear, if it's not asking too much, you might fly down for a week or two and cheer her up. I wish she'd sell the shop."

Tracy shook her head. "Not as long as she can continue with it. Uncle Stanley would haunt her!"

"I know. Even if he was my only brother, I do think he was a very stubborn individual. He practically ate books. Did you know the shop was patterned after one at Stonesgate, an English village about ninety miles from London?"

"Oh, yes, indeed! I can still see the steel engraving of it. It hung immediately over the tea table. Atmosphere, you know. I've been a little hazy about what to do in the next two months. Maybe it would be fun to go down and at least visit Auntie Ellen for a little while, and see if I can reassure her there's business as usual at the shop. Of course she doesn't know there's a general let-down in business, a sort of depression."

"No. Ellen wouldn't know about that.

I'll bet she never listens to anything more than the general news."

"Nothing more than 'Book Chats,' and as for reading, hers consists of the *Saturday Review* and the *Times* reviews, plus, of course, the trade magazines," added Tracy.

"When I remember how she came to me in tears once because Stanley seemed to love books more than her!" Mrs. Allen smiled. "I just can't imagine her ever becoming so steeped in the world of books. I used to think she hated the very word."

"Maybe she did. Maybe she still does, and having to continue the shop is some sort of penance," said Tracy.

"Don't go psychological on me!" moaned her mother.

"I promise! No, she caught the fever. It's incurable."

"What about you?"

"Born with it, I suppose. I'll go to Aunt Ellen's, Mother. I won't promise to have a career, though. After all, there's Bob to consider. He wants to get married in the fall."

The autumn had not been mentioned as

a possible date for their wedding, and Tracy's mother looked surprised.

"I know, Mother, we never could agree on it until now. I still think Bob should finish his Master's before we marry. He insists that his scholarship, with what he can make on the side, will provide enough for us to manage on."

"I feel it's entirely up to you two to decide, Tracy. Your father and I'd love to have you at home another year, of course. We thought you might work in the University Library in the Special Collections, perhaps do research in the State Library."

All of this had been discussed before. Tracy had the word of one of the librarians at the State Library that she would find a place for her in the Research Department. There was also a job downtown as librarian for the largest advertising agency in the city.

What Tracy barely recognized herself, but what her parents had begun to suspect, was the fact that she was not quite ready to marry Bob Follett. There was no great urgency, no excitement at the knowledge that Bob would be calling her within the hour for a date for the evening.

She wore his pin, and she knew that it would be replaced in a short time with his ring. Sometimes she thought bitterly that she wasn't at all certain that she was in love with Bob. How could you be sure?

"If you go to San Francisco, when would you like to leave?" Her mother's query startled Tracy.

When could she leave? There were no pressing engagements, nothing but a luncheon date with Mary Lindsey, her best friend. It was a standing date every Wednesday, to give them a chance to survey the past week end and to plan their next activities. Mary would probably go to Mexico with her parents next month. Actually, the old crowd was breaking up rather quickly now. Two weddings, one European tour and visiting relatives and friends contrived to separate them, so that of the eight girls who had gone through elementary and high school as well as college together, only Tracy and Mary were in town most of the time.

"I'll call Mary. She'll be envious, but of course she's planning on Mexico. Bob won't like my going, but then he should work hard this summer. He's taking a tough course, and I think there's going to be a lot more research than he realizes. He'll do better with me away."

Her mother didn't answer. She was remembering his many papers which Tracy had helped prepare. Bob would probably miss her in more ways than Tracy would admit!

"Your clothes need looking after, I suppose?"

Tracy smiled. "I could take them to the cleaners and have them shipped directly, just taking a few things to start me off."

"Ellen will take you to I. Magnin's before your head's cooled from your hat!"

"I know. She'll insist on my getting a fluffy dinner dress, and I'll buy a knit suit!"

"Susan and Leslie will be envious! Here they come!"

Leslie, her black hair flying, her jeans wet and bedraggled upon her twelve-year-old figure, sauntered over the grass to the patio. "What's cooking?"

"Your fair skin, if it doesn't freckle," said Tracy.

"It's hopeless. Mom, could I have a sandwich? I'm starved. I can't wait until supper, or dinner, or whatever you call it on Sunday."

"Yes, dear. Go in and clean up and fix yourself a ham on rye, if you wish. Don't cut your hand with that big knife. Daddy just sharpened it." Her mother rose from the bench. "I'll go, too; you always make a mess in the kitchen. Did you do a good job on the car?"

"Oh, sure. Sue's just polishing the last window. She wants a sandwich, too. Coming, Trace?"

"Yes, I'll join you. Only I want coffee with mine."

"Maybe I should rush dinner along. I never did hold much with the idea of 'Brunch' on Sunday and one other meal. Your father is a three-meal-a-day man," said Mrs. Allen.

"Yeah, seven, twelve and six," said Leslie. "I'm for it, myself!" She left them at the side door, going in through the utility room.

Entering the big cool kitchen, Tracy could already feel a quick stab of the nostalgia she'd experience for all this when she was in San Francisco.

Their father was a fairly successful

businessman, and they had a comfortable home. Her mother worked too hard, of course, but what mother who had four children wasn't forever busy? They engaged a part-time maid occasionally in the winter, when the busiest entertaining occurred. But Tracy's mother was an excellent housekeeper, taking pride in her home, and loved the hustle and bustle of planning and executing those plans.

"It smells good in here," said Tracy.

"It's the turkey. I always think there's nothing like a ham or a nice turkey for a big family to carve—as long as it lasts."

"Which, of course, isn't too long," added Tracy.

She surveyed the big room with its rows of pale yellow steel cabinets, its built-in ovens, copper kettles hanging in a pattern of bright sunshine. "I'll brew a pot of coffee, and you go see if your father's awake," said her mother.

2

DINNER was to be at seven that evening, and at her father's insistence, Bob Follett would join them. He had called from his fraternity, the Sigmu Nu, which was keeping its doors open to about a dozen students attending summer session.

Tracy had given him no hint of the news she had to tell him. She felt a bit guilty, knowing that she was delaying it as long as possible, and realizing that he wouldn't like her leaving.

As she dressed for the evening, combing her long black hair into a neat, shining pony tail, she thought of the solitude on the plane she would catch tomorrow at Portland, and of the long days to follow when she could think about Bob at a distance.

She tucked the last pin into the deep waves, then picked up the photograph of the handsome young man. Much too good-looking, her brother Tom had said when

14

she withdrew it from its wrappings at Christmas. The family had admired its frame, and the well-chiseled profile. Instinctively, Tracy knew that there was a lack of real warmth among the members of her family toward Bob, although since she was engaged to him, they did try to like him.

She studied his face for a long moment, then abruptly set the picture down again on her dressing table.

There had once been another boy.

She could feel her heart beating more rapidly as she recalled how, when she was sixteen, she had almost tiptoed past his house, fearing, hoping, praying that he would burst from either the front or the side door in time to greet her; trembling in a frenzy of indecision whether to say nonchalantly, "Hi! Jeff," or to pretend she hadn't seen him.

She had cried when his mother died. She had cried again when she'd seen him smoking with a gang of boys a few weeks later, and sobbed to herself, "Poor boy! He wouldn't do that if his mother had lived!"

She looked at herself in the mirror,

wondering if Bob would like the new sack dress she had bought last week. It was not too plain, since it had a Pilgrim collar, and a row of white buttons offset the severity of the straight lines. It was of a new shade of green, and lent a hazel tone to her large grey eyes.

Adding a final touch of her *Certainly Red* lipstick, she once more scrutinized herself critically. Five feet six inches was a fairly respectable height for a girl especially if she dated a six-foot-two man. She sighed a bit. Bob liked her to wear heels on their dates. She kicked off the mules and slipped her slender feet into spike-heeled white kid pumps.

She could hear the chimes ringing, so, dabbing herself with a bit of perfume, she hurried toward the stairs.

Susan, bewitching in a sheer black chiffon, was letting him in. When she was not a tomboy, Susan was a real threat to any girl, Tracy told herself generously. And so she looked there in the hall, her head tilted so that auburn lights danced in it. Her blue eyes shining, her red lips smiling, Susan was a real beauty. Bob was telling her so.

Her own voice startled her as Tracy called, "Hi Bob!"

"Hello, Dream Gal!" Bob grinned up at her.

Susan gave a little flutter with her hands and said, "Oh, I'll run along now that Tracy's ready."

"Don't rush away, Susan. Though how any man can stand being surrounded with so much beauty at one time—" Bob broke off appealingly, spreading his hands.

Leslie, coming in from the kitchen, shrugged a lean shoulder and, out of sight of Bob, clasped her hands across her chest and murmured, "Dear me, Suz!" Going back into the kitchen, she asked the swinging door, "How can she stand him?"

But of course Bob dashing for a touchdown with a ball tucked under his arm was an entirely different man from Bob with the hand of a girl tucked under his arm.

"He's just not real," Leslie further addressed the door. "He's a completely phony stinkeroo."

"Who's what?" Her mother, coming out of the butler's pantry bearing the turkey on the old blue platter, tipped her head quizzically at her youngest.

17

"Oh, Bob. He's great on the football field, but impossible as a suitor."

Her mother smiled at the word *suitor*. Leslie read all kinds of books and listened to all kinds of television programs and loved sports. As a football hero, Bob was tops to Leslie, but at her age of twelve years, she could not accept him in his present role.

"Set the salads on for me?" her mother asked.

"Oh, sure. I don't mind. To the left?"

"Do we always have to go through that? Can't you remember?"

"I guess so. It's awfully silly, anyway. I'll bet everyone could hunt for his own, if he didn't know where it was."

"What you need is a good series of Home Ec courses in high school."

"I'd rather be a scientist, and they're much worse needed."

"Okay, so be a scientist, but do get the salads on. Your father's hungry."

Presently they sat down to dinner in the formal dining room. The large Duncan Phyfe table and the china closet, the lace tablecloth, the fine crystal and bone china, the solid silver and the serving cart bespoke of countless such dinners.

The Allens had always used fine linen napkins for all their evening meals. Mr. Allen, ignoring his daughter's pleas for the as-good-as-linen paper ones, insisted that a house must retain some modicum of formality, and it might as well begin in the dining room.

The table conversation embraced Bob's vacation in Seattle with his parents, their health and their plans for the summer. His father, an appliance salesman, was thinking of opening his own business, and his mother was expecting a summer guest.

"And how does your father feel about your prospective coaching career?"

Bob laughed shortly. "It would be tame. I think he really favors professional football."

"And how do you yourself feel now that you've had a couple of weeks to think it over?"

"I'm not sure. I'd like to finish my Master's, but if I sign with the Coast League, I've got to make up my mind this month."

Tracy would not let her eyes meet

Bob's, although she felt his searchingly upon her. This was something he'd have to decide for himself. She really didn't feel too strongly either way. There'd be a lot of excitement in the professional field, but she knew it would be less permanent than a coaching job.

She suddenly thought of the bookshop waiting for her in San Francisco, and could feel the peace of a quiet afternoon permeate her. Then superimposed on that image was one of fur coats, bronze mums, the blue haze of autumn, Bob hurling himself over the line for a touchdown. The incongruity brought a smile to her lips.

"What's funny, Trace?" asked the unquenchable Leslie.

Tracy shook her head at her. But Bob hadn't noticed, so she was safe enough.

"I'm going to the movies with Dick, Mom," said Susan as she rose to help clear the table for dessert.

"What's playing?" asked Leslie.

"*The Key*. Much too old for you, Leslie," said Susan.

"Who're you to decide?"

"Girls!" admonished their father.

"She always thinks I'm a baby, unless

she wants me to help her do something hard, like washing the station wagon."

"Well, anyway, you wouldn't want to go with me and Dick."

"Certainly not. But there's always Kay and Betts."

"But not tonight, Leslie. You're going on a picnic tomorrow."

"I love these family courts, don't you?" Bob asked in an aside to Tracy.

"Not always, but they do seem necessary." I wish they'd settle these things elsewhere, she thought. Bob must think we're uncivilized. He, being an only child, was unused to having the dinner table serving as a clearing house for family problems.

"How does your father feel about recent developments in the Far East?" her father blessedly came to the rescue.

"He's pretty badly upset, sir. Of course he hasn't had much time to think about it, since he's busy with plans."

"Could make a difference to some of you boys who may be called into service," Mr. Allen observed. "I hate to think of the possibility of there being a shooting war even at that distance."

21

"Makes every one of us a little uneasy."

The frozen dessert interrupted any further discussion, and Tracy felt relieved. She had been old enough during the Korean War to feel its impact, and another war would bring much graver consequences to the whole world.

When they'd finished, she said, "Let us girls clear the table, Mother, and stack things in the dishwasher. You've had quite a day."

"Not tonight, dear. You and Bob run along to the living room. I know you've a lot to discuss."

She knew Bob detected a note of warning in her mother's tone, and was not surprised when he asked her to go for a drive.

She got a shortie from the hall closet, and they went out into the lovely twilight of an Oregon day. The sunset was especially beautiful, and the dark shadows of tall spruce cast their lengths across the velvet green of the grass as they walked toward Bob's convertible.

"What did your mother mean—we've got a lot to talk about?"

"Oh, a letter from my Aunt Ellen, Bob.

I'm thinking of going down to San Francisco for a little while."

"No! Oh, Tracy, you can't do that!" Dismay and indignation struggled for supremacy in his tone. "Summer's just beginning, and we'll have a lot of fun."

"Maybe that's one reason I should go. You ought to put in some good hard work, you know. You have to make up that one course before you can start the fall term."

"It'll be a breeze—with you here to help me with my term paper. But of course if you're away—gosh!" He slowed the car. "Say, do you know, I'm counting on your helping me with it?"

"You can do it easily, Bob. I never felt right about helping you with that Literature paper."

"Why not? It was such a stupid assignment, and you knew all the answers."

"But it was a required course, and you could have done it yourself."

"After all, you helped me only a little!" Bob laughed. She had done most of the work, he very well knew. She pretended that his ideas were good and that, since he knew where to find the references, she had just helped jog his memory.

But she still resented his finally leaving it to her to organize; and in the very end, she had typed it for him. Thirty pages of well written material, with footnotes and bibliography. Just plain cheating, if you ask me, and you're no better than the one you did it for, her conscience shouted at her.

He broke the silence. "All right, go ahead and lecture me, Tracy. I know that I'd never have gotten the scholarship if you'd not helped me last term. It was more than the Lit paper. It was all of the papers you did."

Her father's voice: *"You're overworking. It seems to me that you're doing one term paper right after another. I think you should drop at least one of your courses and finish next year."*

Her mother: *"Tracy, I wasn't the least bit sneaky, nor did I suspect that you were doing Bob's work, too, until you asked me to send that folder to you by Leslie. Naturally, I had to be sure it was the right one, and when I saw the title page with his name on it, ready to hand in, I suddenly realized why you were so overworked all this winter."*

Tracy had been very nervous over all of it. It was something one could be dismissed for. It had been unfair of Bob to ask her to do it for him. He always had such excellent excuses, though. She had never meant to become so involved, and now she knew all that she'd done was cruelly dishonest, besides being unfair to him. Each time she'd objected he'd said, "But I only want you to do just this one little paper, honey. It's nothing I couldn't get a typist to do for me, of course, at a price. And you know that we can use the money for other things."

Suddenly she realized that she'd be very thankful to let Bob take care of his own research this summer. He could either do the work or give up the idea of a Master's Degree. While he might be able to get by with someone else doing most of the research and writing for a term paper, he would be taking two orals and a written examination that he'd need to be prepared for, besides his thesis.

"You wouldn't go away and leave me all alone this summer, now would you, dear?" His hand left the wheel and covered hers tenderly.

She steeled herself. "Yes, Bob, I think I should." He'd never really understand why she had to do this. "You see, Aunt Ellen needs me so terribly. We have our whole lives to spend. She may have such a little time, and I could be of such great help to her."

"But, Tracy, she doesn't need you as much as I do, and after all, we're engaged. You do want to help me, don't you?"

"Oh, Bob, if you mean help you with your courses, the answer, even though you can't see it—is *No*. Can't you see I must not help you with material you'll be tested on?" As though only the fact of his being tested on it were her reason! She felt an overwhelming desire to cry out at him and make him see that he was cheating himself, her and betraying all of the principles of complete honesty.

"Going ethical on me?" his cool voice asked.

"I have certain scruples, although I seem to have forgotten them."

"Guess we just don't see this thing the same way."

"Probably not. Oh, Bob, it's so important to me. You can do the work, and you have to take the examinations. It isn't as though you *couldn't*!"

"And if I couldn't you'd be willing to help me?" he asked playfully. "Simply because I do have the ability, you have not felt you were cheating?"

The ugly word was out in the open. Taking a good long look at herself and at him as well as at the word, Tracy said bitterly, "I knew all along that it was wrong, as you did. If it was found out, we'd both be expelled, as you know. I'm not very proud of myself for having done the work."

"Nor of me for making you do it? Oh, Tracy, for Pete's sake, get off your soap box."

He would never understand. But I do have to live with myself. "Isn't that a beautiful moon?" she asked. She had put her soapbox away now, and she knew how to change to a subject that pleased him.

3

IT was not a very successful date. They were never able to recapture the light feeling of their last one, and so it ended on an unhappy note, with Bob still pleading for her to stay at home and not to go running off to San Francisco.

"When will you come back?" he asked finally.

"I'm not sure, Bob, but probably by the end of July."

"Almost six weeks?"

"The time will fly. You'll see."

"I'll be bored stiff. You know what the Summer session's like. All the teachers back on campus trying to renew life and catch up on courses they've missed." His flat tone indicated his boredom.

"You might find someone you like very much. There are lots of young teachers today, you know."

"Does that mean you'll be finding someone interesting in San Francisco?"

"Bob, we're almost quarreling."

"Well, does it?" he insisted.

"Please don't be like that. You know I've never had a date with another man since you gave me your pin."

"It should be a ring before you leave. Meet me at D'Arcy Jewelers tomorrow noon?"

"I can't, Bob. I'm leaving at ten for Portland."

Later, as she brushed her hair and got ready for bed, she remembered his kiss on her lips. It seemed distant and cool, compared to their usual good nights.

He really is angry with me, and I can't say I blame him too much, Tracy thought. She went over by her open window, knelt down on the soft green carpeting and, leaning her head on her hands, drank in the late night air. A fragrance of roses drifted up to her. The dark firs rose in a straight column to the left, outlining the edge of their lawn, and she could hear the tinkling of the small brook which Tom had engineered into a waterfall and pool when he was a Freshman in high school. He had also put in a small water wheel to generate electricity with which he powered an electric train. It had taken all kinds of mechanical skill to get it to work, and even his teacher had come out to see it.

When it was exhibited at the Science Fair at the State College in the spring, he had taken a blue ribbon, and all of it had contrived to further his interest in Engineering, so that he hoped to get two years at MIT.

My family, thought Tracy, are probably like other girls' families, but it has always seemed to me they're sort of special. I'll get homesick, but I'm not coming back for a weekend, even if Aunt Ellen insists on it, until I see that she's reassured about the bookshop.

At that moment she heard Tom's jaloppy entering the drive. There was no mistaking it, of course. It thundered up the paving and on into its stall in the garage, lights and motor dying simultaneously. For all the racket he made getting home, he came up the stairs wondrously quietly. Tracy smiled. He avoided the creaking stair which their father playfully said was his signal so he'd know what time they got in.

Throwing her robe about her, she stepped out into the hall and whispered to

30

her brother, "Hey! How about a lemonade or something?"

"Okay. I could eat a sandwich," agreed Tom.

They went quietly down the back stairs to the kitchen, closing the hall door.

"It's like saying 'Sh!' to an explosion, after your car's awakened the neighborhood," laughed Tracy. "I wonder there've not been complaints."

"They'd have to pull in a lot of jaloppies. Most of the kids own worse ones than mine. Everybody's gotten used to 'em!"

Tracy set out cold ham and a pitcher of lemonade. She got out bread, pickles and mayonnaise and went to work. "How was the picnic? And did you take Tamara?"

"Fine picnic. I didn't take Tam. I took Jeanne instead."

"Oh?"

"Tam's in LA. Jeanne's pretty cute; she'll do until Tam gets back." So simple.

Tom, at twenty, was the image of his father. Tall, lean and dark-haired with the Allen physical characteristics, he resembled his sister. All the Allen children had good features, with straight noses, dimples in their chins, fair complexions with a tendency to high red cheek bones. The whole tribe was nice to look upon, Ellen Taylor used to say when she came up from San Francisco to visit.

Tracy told her brother of her impending departure.

"Gad! That's sudden, isn't it?" Tom took a bite of ham on rye. "What did Bob think?"

Tracy shrugged a slim shoulder. "Not so pleased, of course."

"Why should he be? This town's pretty dead in the summer."

"Not necessarily. There are parties at the Country Club, and swimming in several private pools."

"Gee, I think it will be fun in 'Frisco!" Tom drank his lemonade. "I'll be slaving away at the paper mill, trying to make a few bucks to run the jaloppy and pay my fees next term. Guess that's better than being stuck in a bookshop all day, though."

"But I love books. Remember?"

"See you at early breakfast?"

"Probably. I'll pack and get ready. I called Aunt Ellen this afternoon and asked her to meet my plane. She was so relieved. I'm hoping she won't be disappointed."

"She's probably lonesome, living in that big place with Uncle Stanley gone."

"Well, we'd better call it a day. See you in the morning."

Her mother and her two sisters took her to the airport the next day. The usual rush of the tourist season had filled every seat, and she had been able to get a ticket only because someone had canceled just before she called in.

"Do you want a round trip ticket, miss? Better make your return reservation now, if you're planning on coming back this summer," observed the agent.

"I don't know when I'll return, so just the one I reserved yesterday, please," she answered.

If I get stuck I can come by train, or Bob might even drive down for me, she thought.

They had only a half-hour wait, and the other two girls went to watch planes coming in and taking off from the field. She and her mother discussed a few details concerning her clothes and social activities that Tracy would be unable to attend.

As she boarded the big airliner, Tracy felt the surge of excitement attendant upon departures by plane. She was lucky to get a seat from which she could wave to her family, and see the neatly patterned landscape as they left the airport, flying low enough to see river and ships, trees and houses.

Then they were in the clouds, and she leaned her head back, grateful for a chance to think about her next few weeks in San Francisco.

Aunt Ellen, a trim, sophisticated figure in a dark silk suit topped with a small fur cape, was waiting for her at the gate as she came forward after the plane landed. Her blue eyes shining with delight at seeing her pretty niece, Ellen Taylor kissed her fondly and drew her inside the lobby of the terminal building.

"Did you have lunch on the plane? It's a little early yet, but you know it would be fun to go to the Pancake Palace."

"I'd love that. We had coffee about an hour's flight away from Portland, but I could eat some blueberry pancakes."

Ellen nodded. "It's a pleasant place. I

always like to come here. We can get your luggage later."

It was different now, without Uncle Stanley to look after details. In a way, Tracy supposed, that was one reason they must go to the Pancake Palace. They must break the pattern of tradition as it was in the old days. You'd never have been able to get Uncle Stanley into a pancake place! "Typical woman food, with all that feminine atmosphere and fancy berry sauces."

"I notice men lap it up too, and pronounce it good, when they come in from waiting for planes or landing."

"Only to tide 'em over till steaks are available," her husband would say.

He had been gone too short a time yet for her not to miss him, Tracy thought as she realized he was not just around the corner getting the luggage checks taken care of.

But Aunt Ellen was valiant about it. She had broken down completely at Christmas time, having come North for the holidays.

At their small table, Aunt Ellen ordered for them, and Tracy observed the small cart bearing different syrups and berries and fruits being passed among the guests.

She leaned over and patted her aunt's hand. "I'm really hungry. Guess I was too excited to eat this morning. I just drank some juice and coffee."

"We'll have dinner about five, dear. Lucy is roasting a leg of lamb. She's so pleased you're to be with us."

It must be rugged cooking for only Aunt Ellen and herself. Tracy recalled the veteran housekeeper whom she had known through the years. There was a maid, too, and there had been a gardener and chauffeur at one time, but now only a part-time gardener took care of the grounds.

They arrived at the large stone house about three o'clock, and Tracy looked across the wide marine drive at the sparkling waters of the Bay. A small sailing vessel scudded across the smooth surface, and several fishing boats were visible in the distance. The tranquility of the scene always amazed her. Such a big city, and this such a quiet, restful place! Uncle Stanley had inherited it from his father, who had been a shipping magnate. The house was one of the few which stood alone in its grounds in this area, many of the earlier ones having been converted to flats or apartments.

The stone was of a creamy color, and the house boasted wide green shutters at its big windows, a red tile roof, and shrubs and trees from the corners of the earth. Ignoring the century of progress the marine drive had known, the house was of the sort one might find in New Orleans, with its lacy ironwork outlining a balcony and the lower piazza.

Aunt Ellen drove the handsome black car up to the side entrance and parked. "Just come on in, and I'll send Mattie out for the bags. Honestly, if you weren't here, I'd be tempted to let her go, there's so little for her to do. But Stanley wouldn't like that, of course."

"Naturally. Besides, I think Mattie is good for you, Aunt Ellen." On her day off, Mattie scoured the city passionately loving each little crooked street and each hill. She always came back to the house loaded with various things she had accumulated. She'd ride the cable cars, walk up Russian Hill, eat at the newest restaurant at Fisherman's Wharf, and come home with stars in her eyes.

Mattie was down the stairs in a flash, as soon as they entered the wide front door. A dark, trim woman of thirty-two, she had worked for the Taylors for ten years and kept the upstairs immaculate. Lately she had been helping Lucy with the kitchen work and the downstairs, and Ellen knew that she wanted to stay on.

"Did you have a good trip, Miss Tracy?" asked Mattie. "Wasn't it exciting to fly?"

"Yes, Mattie. I always enjoy flying. It's a beautiful day."

"All days in San Francisco are beautiful," said Mattie.

"Even with the fog?"

"Even with the fog. Even when the rain's pouring straight down." Mattie, who had married, had lost her GI in World War II, come over to the States from England and would always love America. Once a house servant in England, she appreciated the newer appliances and the warmth of the big house on the Bay.

She went to get the luggage while Tracy went out to the kitchen to pay her respects to Lucy, who was cleaning celery at the

38

sink. She wiped her hands and shook Tracy's hand heartily.

"It's time some of you came down to look after your aunt." She smiled to take the accusing tone from the words. "She's been so worried over that bookshop! I wished all last week that she'd sell it."

"Sh! She might hear you, Lucy," admonished the girl, hastily looking toward the kitchen hallway.

"I already told her what I think about it," placidly said Lucy, from the security of a thirty-year position with the family. "But she didn't listen to me. She can't sleep nights. Mattie and I hear her up roaming around the house night after night, bothering her pretty head with pages of figures, and she not needin' to. Mr. Taylor wouldn't have wanted her to worry so, even if he would turn over in his grave if she sold it."

Tracy nodded. "I don't know what good I'll be. But maybe just having one of the family here will be some help to her."

"Anyway, I'm glad it's you who came, Miss Tracy."

39

Going upstairs with Mattie and her luggage, Tracy had misgivings about the whole plan. After all, I don't know much about merchandising!

Mattie preceded her down the hall to the room which she'd always occupied, and Tracy, entering, felt the thick pile of the lovely Chinese rug beneath her feet, saw the delicate blue and white of the antique satin spread and drapes and her favorite rose coverlet spread over the pink chaise. Two demure little rockers stood near the four windows overlooking the Bay, and the desk top was shining in its usual mahogany splendor. The graceful corner what-not still held the little figurines which had been the love of her girlhood, a Dresden shepherdess and a small flock of white lambs. A gleaming gold and dark clock from Vienna with musical notes had entranced her one Christmas holiday. Mattie began to unpack for her while Tracy went over to the bookcases and observed the treasures she had been presented with during visits in San Francisco. Duplicates had been sent to the family home, so that these remained intact in a collection for all three of the Allen girl children.

Tracy's hands lovingly touched the beautiful bindings. *Alice In Wonderland, The Wind in The Willows, Grimm's Fairy Tales,* Andersen, *Five Little Peppers, Anne of Green Gables,* the *Little Colonel* books, *Secret Garden, Heidi, Roller Skates,* which she had cried over copiously, *Little Women, Jo's Boys, Hans Brinker, Stories of the Operas, Ferdinand,* and more and more. Down through the shelves she went. Her hand stopped, and she took out a new one. Of course! Its duplicate had reached them last December. *Eloise!* They had taken turns reading it to each other on Christmas Eve amid gales of laughter and some tears, remembering it was the last book that Uncle Stanley had chosen for them. It now graced Leslie's own private book shelf.

She pulled the book out and turned to the fly leaf. The shaking finger had lovingly set down the inscription, "To The Allen Girls, Dear Little Tracy, Susan and Leslie, from your adoring Uncle Stanley and Auntie Ellen. Merry Christmas, Dears!"

A tear slipped down Tracy's cheeks. *Dear Little Tracy!* She had always been the little mite climbing upon his knee to hear another story from his inexhaustible supply.

4

AFTER dinner Ellen and Tracy had a quiet little talk about the shop. Her aunt spoke calmly today, although yesterday when she had called about her plane, Tracy had detected the same uneasiness which Ellen's letter had shown.

"Just knowing that you are coming helped to settle my nerves, dear. Honestly, I've been so upset. Mr. Kennedy would like to buy the shop, but he doesn't show any signs of having money with which to pay for it. I'm sure that I could get a much better offer if I were to advertise it, say in the *Saturday Review*, or a trade magazine."

"But you don't really want to sell it, do you?"

"No, of course not! I've come to love the place dearly. I've even asked Mr. Kennedy to start serving tea again, although that was one of the first services he discontinued. Said it always was so much trouble, having the caterer bringing in the tea things. Said it disrupts business!" Ellen said indignantly.

"It was an unusual tradition," Tracy said. She added hastily, "But it was a very pleasant one. I'm sure that it cost Uncle Stanley much more than you realized, and maybe the new manager thinks it's too much to add to overhead."

"Pooh! He just doesn't want to bother with it. I'd like to begin again with the custom, say about twice or three times a week. It gives some of the girls a place to meet when they're exhausted from shopping. You know the Lane is very close to the Square, just a short step from Magnin's and Gump's. In the old days many of our friends would come to the shop instead of the lobby of the St. Francis or the Mark."

"Competition, I remember."

Aunt Ellen laughed. "Not really! But we did get some interesting authors now and then. I remember C. Y. Lee, *The Flower Drum Song* author, was our last guest of honor at an autographing party. Stanley admired him so much. He was very popular, and now his book's to be made into a musical. Just goes to show you that Stanley did know how to recognize a good book!"

"How are the rare books coming these days? I remember Mrs. Gretchen Koch used to buy two a year for the Historical Library."

"Yes, indeed! See, I knew you'd remember some of the details!" Her aunt smiled. "Mrs. Koch called Saturday afternoon and said that she must be making her selection right away. I disliked calling Mr. Kennedy about it, but you can discuss it with him this week. Maybe you could go through that list of rarities we have and help her select one. She seems to favor the Civil War."

"Of course. That's because her grandfather was a plantation owner on the James River."

"At ninety it matters more," agreed Aunt Ellen.

"She's given a lot of books to the Historical Library, and I think she should be allowed to choose the subject."

"Oh, she picks a variety. I know there's a first edition of *Paradise Lost*, and one of

Shakespeare's Folios, that she chose last year."

"Aunt Ellen, tell me about Marcia. Why did Blair Kennedy let her go?"

"He said that she just doesn't know enough about the book business. Stanley wouldn't have liked that. She'd been with us five years, and was always so charming at the tea table. She knew most of our older clients and was so impressive with her quiet dignity. And by the way she handled the stock, anyone could see that she truly loved and appreciated good books."

"Of course! I hope she was able to get a good position?"

"Certainly. I gave her a letter to the Bancroft Library, and one to the Special Collections at the University of Lower California. I haven't heard from her recently, but she had accepted a position as assistant to the Special Collections Librarian, at the Asbury Library. It carries prestige, even though they do not pay quite as well as Stanley."

"And tell me about the new man at the shop."

"Miles Stewart. Well qualified, I

presume, although I've never had a chance really to visit with him. Two men in the shop! We need a woman's touch. I can't get down more than twice a week, dear. I really haven't been feeling too well. And, frankly, Blair Kennedy is not as pleasant as I used to find him when Stanley was there."

Tracy went to bed feeling disturbed over the whole situation, but still not knowing what she could do to better things.

If Marcia, who had been with her uncle for five years, could not please the manager, how could she possibly hope to?

At her aunt's insistence, she slept late on Tuesday, and they made a foray on Magnin's in the early afternoon, after lunching at the Sir Francis Drake.

"Darling, there's a new shipment of Italian knits I want you to see. You'd look perfectly entrancing in one of them, if you can find your color," her aunt had begun at dessert.

So they were shown the new knits and, of course, Tracy was beguiled into buying one of them.

"But I'll not put it on your charge account, Aunt Ellen."

"Don't be like that, Tracy. It isn't even a gift. It's a bonus for coming on down to San Francisco just when I need you most."

"You don't get bonuses for work you haven't done yet," objected Tracy. "I don't really begin to earn anything until I punch the time clock!"

"I can't imagine a time clock at the Book Nook on Dunleith Lane."

They laughed; the sound was a pleasant note in the dressing room. "The sack!" said Tracy, turning around once more to see the beautiful green fabric from a free-flowing back. "Shall I belt it?"

"Not with that lissome figure!" said her aunt. "You need a tiny hat to go with it. It'll be just right for some evening dates, and even for the first tea that you will inaugurate at the shop."

"You will insist then?"

"Yes, I think so. We'll get out little invitations on our own gilt-edged cards. It will please the customers no end, especially since it's summer and there's not too much going on."

"I expect we'll need to work it out."

"I'll just tell Mr. Kennedy that I expect to initiate the teas again the first week in

July. We should be able to get an interesting author to autograph for us. I'll call the Doubleday editor and see if they have a new book off the press."

"The ALA is meeting here about the third week of July."

"The Caldecott and Newberry award dinner! The very thing! And a Poetry Festival this year at San Jose State! See, dear! You'd make a good public relations man!"

"I just happen to have read about it in the *New York Times'* Book Section last week."

"I should have had a notice from the shop! I asked Mr. Kennedy to let me know any time there's anything exciting going on in the world of books in the city." Two lines appeared between Ellen's brows. "I might have missed this entirely. Now it's up to you, dear, to hunt us up an exciting author. Maybe we could get one or two more, and have two successive teas."

"We'll see. Here's the salesgirl coming now with the package. Thank you," she said, holding out her hand. "I know I'll enjoy wearing the dress."

The petite salesgirl wore a happy expression. "You look simply lovely in it, Miss Allen. Come back soon."

"Magnin's is a habit," Tracy said, "one that I mustn't get too soon." But handsome clothes, simple and warm, were almost a must in San Francisco. And in her new work, Tracy must be well groomed and ready to meet her aunt's admiring clientele.

Businesslike, she rose early and breakfasted from a tray in her room, between her bath and dressing for the shop. Her aunt had planned to take her into the city to the shop, but was suffering from a headache, and Tracy refused to let her get up.

"Why, I'll simply catch the bus from the next corner. I'm used to walking miles, or taking any old transportation available. It'll be just fine for me to go by myself."

However, a little later, when she walked into the shop and the thin young man she recognized at once as the new manager greeted her, she wasn't so sure.

He must have just opened the place, she realized, although it was a few minutes after nine-thirty, her uncle's usual opening time. He seemed a little surprised, but smiled and said, "Can I help you?"

"I'm Tracy Allen," she said simply.

"How do you do, Miss Allen. I'm Blair Kennedy. Have you something special you're interested in?"

"Why, I—" She broke off at the abrupt ringing of the telephone.

"Excuse me? Browse around, or wait in there, if you like," Kennedy called, going into his private office. The door swung to after him.

She glanced at the cheerful-looking small room to which he'd motioned. Faltering a little, she entered it, and sank down on the leather chair near the door. She glanced idly at the shelves.

Aunt Ellen hasn't told him about my coming to work! the amazing thought flashed through her mind. Gee! That puts me in a rough spot. And isn't that just like Aunt Ellen? But she did mean to bring me in and introduce me, and then couldn't. She's forgotten all about it, of course, not realizing that he didn't know I'm coming in.

The outer door opened and another young man entered. This one was about twenty-five or so. He took off his hat and hung it on a small rack near a side door, and for a moment Tracy could study him. His auburn hair was very dark, but under the lights she could see the sparkle of reddish coloring. As he turned toward her suddenly, an expression of surprise flitted across his face, too. He nodded pleasantly and then turned to the long table near the center of the room and worked on the display.

He thinks I'm a customer, too, waiting for Mr. Kennedy.

Tracy looked at the collection of books nearest her. They were old and rare. Very good, very unusual volumes, she was sure. Taking down a large book near her, she was delighted with the binding and the illustrations. Turning to the publisher, she noted the imprint of a very old London firm and, examining the print and the paper, realized that she held in her hand a book probably valued at several hundred dollars.

A little surprised at their being open to the general public, she looked at some of the other volumes. *The door should be locked, and certainly I should not have been allowed to come in here unattended.*

At that moment the young man in the main bookstore came to the door of the small anteroom.

"Is Mr. Kennedy helping you?"

"Yes. He's at the telephone." She indicated the book in her hand. "This is a handsome book. It must be very valuable."

The man's brown eyes lit up. "It is a most unusual book. Are you interested in rare collections, Miss—?"

"I'm Tracy Allen. I'm afraid my arrival is a surprise to both you and Mr. Kennedy. My Aunt Ellen meant to bring me down."

He made a quick effort to hide his ignorance of her kinship. "I'm Miles Stewart, Miss Allen. I really should recognize the name, because I've found reference to you and other members of your family in some of the files."

"Mr. Kennedy didn't seem to recognize the name, and the telephone rang just as I came in—" Her voice was apologetic.

"He's very busy," said Miles Stewart.

"Is there something, Miss Allen, I can help you with?"

Tracy felt a sudden desire to run from the room, and then she noted the young man's friendly smile. He has a few freckles! she thought incongruously. "I hardly know what to say. Aunt Ellen was sick this morning, so I told her I could come in by myself. It has just occurred to me that neither of you knew I was to come in. She didn't talk to you about my helping out?"

Amazement flitted across his face, but again he quickly recovered. "No. But then, of course, she probably discussed it with Mr. Kennedy. He's been quite rushed all last week, and he didn't have a chance to talk with me about anything. Here he comes now. Would you like me to tell him first?" he added kindly.

"No, thank you. I can tell him, although I do think it would have been best—" She broke off as Kennedy came in. "I don't believe you know me, Mr. Kennedy. I'm Mrs. Taylor's niece from Oregon. She had asked me to come down to San Francisco to help out in the shop a while. She couldn't come down this morning."

Disbelief gave way to forced calm. "Oh, really? I'm completely unaware of any change in the management." His cold voice chilled Tracy.

He's simply furious. Oh, dear! Aunt Ellen should have saved me this embarrassment.

"And just what would she like you to do?"

He gave a nod of dismissal to Miles Stewart, who eased himself through the door and out into the main salesroom.

Tracy's head lifted and her chin jutted out a bit. "I'm sorry if this takes you by surprise, Mr. Kennedy. But surely you'll be glad to have some help, if you're as busy as you seem."

"Competent help! Miss Allen, did you say? What makes you qualified to help operate a bookshop? As manager, I do like to choose my help, of course." His tone had changed, and she felt a stab of remorse that she hadn't asked her aunt how the new manager would feel about her helping out. But, naturally, she had presumed that all of the details had been worked out.

Quietly, she told Kennedy of her experience as a student librarian, as a clerk at the University Bookshop for the past two years, her additional experience during two summers here at the Book Nook on Dunleith Lane. "Besides that," she said, a little defensively, "I love books, and have lived with them constantly since I was a child. I know bindings and I can recognize rare books; for instance, the ones in this room. I'm a little surprised to find it open to the public."

"Oh! Well, after all, you are Mrs. Taylor's niece. This is out of bounds for the ordinary customer, naturally." The smooth quality of his tone placated the average client, she supposed, although there was a hint of steel beneath it.

"These books—some of them—are on their way to the vaults, of course." He motioned toward the small closet. "Would you like to hang your coat and hat in there? I'll see what I can drum up for you to do. How about marking prices on some of the new books?"

Tracy experienced a sinking feeling. But after all, that was part of the job. The routine, drab necessities along with the glamour!

She nodded pleasantly. "Whatever you

say. But I do think you should know that I can help in book selection, too. I've served as consultant for juvenile literature for several workshops in the state. Oregon —I mean."

A lift of his brow, a lift of one side of his lips. "Lists are available for that sort of thing, too; you know, 'One Hundred Best Books,' et cetera."

She refrained from answering, took off her suit jacket and her little pert hat, and indicated that she was ready to work.

5

AS though to wear her down and make her dissatisfied with her job, Blair Kennedy seemed to hunt the most disagreeable tasks possible that first two weeks. He decided that a new room should be incorporated for the juvenile books they sold, and so an old storeroom was prepared. Armed with smock, pail and scrub brushes, Tracy cleaned shelves and broke fingernails, tore her hose on boxes, soiled her pretty clothes, rose under a sharp-edged cabinet to get a severe bump on her temple which produced a nagging headache. Still she toiled on bravely, recognizing the tactics, yet ignoring them.

"It does look wonderful," she sighed the evening she finished putting all the new books on the shelves. The colorful jackets were so entrancing. She could stop at any given moment and read for hours the lovely bright books produced for the youth of America.

"Yes, it does, indeed!" agreed Miles

Stewart, coming in at the moment she started admiring her handiwork. "If it weren't for the last smudge you've added to your chin, you'd look more than wonderful."

"I'm exhausted, but I'd never let Mr. Kennedy hear me say so."

"It's five o'clock and time the shop closed. How about a cup of java at the little shop next door?"

"I'd love it, but I'm not fit for public view. Let me clean up a bit first."

"Right. I'll just finish clearing my desk and then I'll take you home, too."

"How nice. I don't think I could step upon a bus or hang to a strap tonight."

She washed up a bit, powdered her nose, added a touch of lipstick and took off the bedraggled smock which she had worn for the past two days. "Ugh!" she said, rolling it into a paper bag to take it home to be laundered. She surveyed her white blouse and shook her head. Sleeveless, and with a small round collar, it had been well covered by the smock, but was not fresh-looking. She buttoned her gray suit jacket up to her throat and pulled on a small white panne velvet hat. Slipping out of her flats, she pushed her narrow feet into slim white pumps. Producing white gloves from the tote bag she carried, she went out to the main salesroom.

Kennedy had just come up from the basement storage room, his arms full of large, heavy volumes. "Oh, still here, Miss Allen? I wonder if you could stay late tomorrow night? I have some orders going out. You can type, can't you?"

"Why, yes. Yes, I'll be glad to stay to help out."

"You must know that the staff usually works one or two nights a week. There's no time and a half, of course; just straight salary."

"I understand."

"Well, maybe you'd eat in town and not count on going home. You can pick up a bite at the coffee shop next door."

"I'll manage all right. Ready?" she asked Miles.

"Yes. Well, good night, Mr. Kennedy. See you in the morning."

"Oh, yes. But, Stewart, I was planning on asking you for some help for another hour or so. But of course if you are going out—"

"Just for coffee. I could come back after I drop Miss Allen by her house."

"I need you now. Of course you could take ten for coffee."

"All right. I'll be right back, then." As they walked around the corner, Miles said to her, "Just my luck, too, right after asking to take you home."

"There'll be another time. I can take the next bus."

"You understand?"

"Oh, certainly." Of course I understand, a lot more than Mr. Kennedy realizes. Hot tears sprang into her eyes and she turned her head deliberately so that Miles wouldn't see them.

They sat in a booth and sipped their hot coffee slowly. She could feel the soothing warmth steal over her and felt happy at Miles' nice solicitous voice.

"I'm sorry about your working so hard, Tracy. Gee! It's not like this all the time. You've done a swell job on the juvenile books. I think the room is going to help business a lot. Those handsome posters and other display materials add an attractive touch."

"While I was putting up the last row of

books, I had an idea to stimulate trade," she confided.

"Like what?"

"Like what my mother did for two years in the public library back home. She held a Children's Story Hour on Saturday afternoons from one-thirty to two-thirty. Sometimes the kids dramatized the stories, and they enjoyed them so much. The crowd soon got so big they had to use an auditorium."

"That's the trouble, probably. We'd grow out of the juvenile room in no time."

"Well, then, maybe we could move to a library somewhere."

"It's a wonderful idea. You could introduce new books to them."

"And have one or two brief reviews from the kids themselves."

"What are we waiting for?"

"Until I get into Mr. Kennedy's good graces."

"It's not really your fault. It would have been better if your aunt had prepared him for your coming."

Tracy shook her head. "I'm not so sure. He'd only have objected to it. This way he could hardly say no without making an issue of the whole thing."

"You're darned good help! We've needed someone very badly. I don't think you should start out being a typist-clerk, though. And someone else could have scrubbed the shelves. It's all right for you to lend your ideas and to arrange the books, but I don't think you need to play janitor."

"I felt a little abused myself, but then I thought perhaps a janitor's wages might be rather high, too!"

"You're kidding! Not compared to your salary. At least I hope that he's paying you what you're worth. Anyone can tell that you know books."

"I don't mind. And now your ten minutes are up and I have to hurry to catch the right bus. Thanks for your kind thoughts, and I'll see you in the morning."

Riding along on the packed bus, Tracy was almost too tired to think about the situation at the shop.

Kennedy was busy all day, of course. He always seemed loaded with work any time that she happened to go to his office. Miles also seemed very busy with customers, coming and going and asking questions. There were several features of great interest to her. One was the fact that book reviewers from the *Chronicle* and the *Examiner* were constantly watching for the most interesting books to use in their columns.

Once a week there was a radio program, "Book Chats," and a school program on television, "What's New In Children's Books," on Saturday mornings. The latter was a round table discussion held by several youngsters and a leading school librarian.

Tracy hoped that some day she'd be called upon to help make the selection. She had been delighted to learn that Robert McCloskey was one of this year's award winners, because she had long been one of his greatest admirers.

She was glad that Miles Stewart had liked the idea of having a story hour at the shop. She'd be very careful about the introduction of the idea to Mr. Kennedy. He had conceded that having afternoon teas at the shop would be beneficial, but they would have only one each week.

Beginning with this week of the

American Library Association Convention, during which time they had been able to secure not one but three authors to drop in at tea time, the plan would continue throughout the remainder of the summer at least.

"We'll see how it works," Kennedy had told Aunt Ellen. "But you must realize that just because an old custom pleased your clients and friends, it doesn't necessarily keep the shop operating on a businesslike level. The cost doesn't balance the advantage, you see. However, if Miss Allen will help, I'm sure that we can help cut those costs enough to have one tea each week, say, perhaps on Thursday afternoons?"

"Right. That's the day, too, that stores stay open, and it does give one a chance for a breather," Miles had observed.

She reached her aunt's house tonight about six o'clock and went straight to her room for a quick bath and to slip into a quilted housecoat for a tray in her room.

"I think I'll go right to bed after I've written a few letters," she said to her aunt who tapped at her door.

"Dear, you look exhausted! You'd

better stay home tomorrow and rest! I didn't mean for you to work so hard. You were to get into the swing of it gradually, remember?"

"I'll admit that I worked steadily, but I did get through with my big project this week." She told her aunt briefly about the children's room. Then, inspired by her aunt's interest, she added briefly the suggestion about the story hour.

"Why, that's just wonderful! How soon can we do it? Oh, dear! I'm as bad as Mr. Kennedy. We won't do it right away. Give yourself another month, and then we can think about it."

Tracy laughed. The whole world of books was so thrilling one idea led to another, until a chain reaction set in and you lived, ate and dreamed of books.

After her shower she felt rested, and so, dressing in a simple gingham plaid dress, she joined her aunt at dinner in the dining room. It was lonely for the older woman, of course, and then, too, Lucy liked people to appreciate her fine meals.

After dinner they went to the lovely living room which tonight had its French doors opened to the rose garden and patio just outside. The sun was going down in a blaze of red and orange; and, stepping out to the patio, the two women could see the small fishing fleet riding at anchor.

Mattie appeared in the doorway. "Telephone, Miss Tracy!"

"Take it in the den if you wish, dear," said Aunt Ellen.

To her great surprise, it was Miles Stewart.

"Tracy? If you've forgiven me sufficiently, and have rested a bit, I wondered if you'd like to take in a show?"

She hesitated. Her thoughts flew instantly to Bob Follett. He had written her three times each week, but to her dismay the letters had all sounded like duty letters. He was obviously still angry with her for having gone to San Francisco for the summer.

Throwing discretion to the winds, she answered, "I'd like that very much, Miles. Thank you."

"Say in about an hour, then? We might go dancing afterwards."

"I'd love that," she agreed.

You didn't need to seem quite so eager, her conscience whispered as she replaced the receiver. But neither need I seem cold to the invitation.

A pang of dismay swept through her as she went to tell her aunt. Of course Ellen had expected Tracy to spend the evening with her. But she had also expressed regret that she knew no young men to introduce her to. Tracy, feeling a bit uneasy about Bob, hadn't told her they were engaged.

"If it's all right, Auntie Ellen, I'm going to a show and maybe dancing afterward, with Miles."

"How nice, dear! I've been hoping you'd find some congenial young man soon. I know it's been lonely."

"Oh, no! I've been too busy," Tracy protested.

They chatted about ten minutes longer, and then Tracy went upstairs to get ready for her date.

It seemed very strange to be going out with someone other than Bob; she'd dated no other boy since they'd begun going out together.

There was a little nagging insistent

thought as she began brushing her hair. If she went out with Miles, she would have to tell Bob. They had a special agreement on that.

6

THEY went to see *Gigi*. Bob Follett had tried in vain to get tickets in Portland, and when Tracy found that Miles had secured two tickets several days before, she felt a bit disloyal. He must have known that she'd go. Or, she told herself, perhaps she was second choice.

It didn't really matter, she decided, just so long as she did get to see it, and suddenly she realized that she was having a wonderful time with Miles.

They went to the Top O' The Mark afterward and stood for a long moment looking out over San Francisco before taking their table near the big windows to the right of the doors.

He ordered for her, and they promised that they'd not say a word about shop tonight. It was a promise easily kept, Tracy found as they went on to talk about their early lives.

"How did you ever get so interested in b-o-o-k-s?" She spelled it out.

70

He laughed at her trick in avoiding shop *talk*. "I got a broken collar bone and was out as far as football was concerned my second year in high school. I began to help out in the library, and the next thing I knew I was a confirmed carrier of packages, opener up of boxes, and putter-on-the-shelves man. Naturally I read a few titles, to see what went where. The next year I worked longer hours and liked it so well that when I entered college I applied for a job in the school library. It helped pay my tuition."

"I love the campus at Stanford," she offered.

He nodded. "It's my favorite home away from home. I took all the literature courses and all the library work possible. I may go into research sometime."

"Or buy a bookshop of your own?"

"Why, yes! How did you guess?"

"Sh! Very close to shop talk, you know."

He had managed to play enough football so that he belonged to the first string the last two years in college, but he hadn't considered it a possible vocation. Remembering Bob's desire either to coach or go

71

into professional football, Tracy was surprised that Miles had considered the book business.

"Don't get me wrong. I love the game, especially when someone else is playing it and I'm in the stadium watching. And I'm not afraid, either. I just happen to like books better."

She nodded. "I can understand that." One didn't have to play football to be held high in her esteem.

"By the way, I thought if you'd like I'd get some tickets to some of the Stanford games next fall."

She felt a little thrill tingle through her. "Gee! That would be fun! Oh, but maybe I won't be here!" How could she have forgotten so soon? After all, she had thought she'd stay just a few weeks, only long enough to reassure her aunt about the shop.

"Of course you'll be here!" protested Miles. "If I ever saw a dedicated person, it's you. Who else would have pitched in and scrubbed old billy out of that dirty storeroom but you? Who else would have lined up all those books with tender loving care but one Tracy Allen?"

"Shop talk! Pay a dime, sir!"

"Oh, well, it's worth it. But you'll be here, I'm sure. His statement was so final that she opened her large grey eyes wider and smiled agreement.

"You're probably right. I've begun to think things are piling up so fast that I couldn't leave if I wanted to."

"Right! And now, do you want to go and dance?"

"Where shall we go? I've not danced for about four weeks. You'll probably have to drag me about the floor."

"Yes, I can imagine that." He helped her with a small fur cape, courtesy Aunt Ellen's wardrobe, and they left the room followed by admiring glances.

They walked a short distance to a night club, and Tracy realized that here was no *gauche* boy. He knew how to get a table, what to order, and how to ask her to dance, all without a trace of awkwardness.

She looked lovely tonight, wearing a pretty full-skirted cotton sheer which floated beguilingly as they danced. The deep full-blown roses of a gorgeous blue with touches of green enhanced her coloring. She was slender and dark and beautiful, but entirely unaware that many compliments were being paid her and the tall thin young man who escorted her. He had been able to get out in the sun last weekend, and so some of the freckles she had noted the first day were now covered with a very slight tan. His auburn hair was molded against his well shaped head like a cap, and his features were strong and clean.

By the time they'd danced an hour they had discovered they were almost perfect partners. Not once did Tracy let herself think of Bob Follett.

By the end of the evening they knew quite a great deal about each other.

Miles lived with his family, which consisted of a brother younger than he, in his first year of college, a sister in high school, and his parents. They lived at Mill Valley across the Bay, where he drove home every night. "Partly to save board and room, though I pay it to Mom instead; partly just because I like to live there. You must come over sometime and see our place, Tracy. It's one of the older houses, and is out at the edge of the city limits,

74

overlooking a hill. We've added a sun deck, and we can look over the entire valley."

"Sounds very interesting. I'd like to come sometime."

"Karen would enjoy you. She's just the age to get a crush on someone like you. And she'd certainly like your sister, Susan."

"Gee! We do know quite a lot about each other after one short evening," said Tracy.

"There's one thing more that I have to know, though I can't imagine any answer but one. Is there another man in your life?"

"Oh!" Why did he have to ask? At least, she amended, why did he have to ask tonight?

"I see. It would be silly, of course, to think there wouldn't be. That's what I meant when I said there could be only one answer. Is it serious?"

"It was serious. Now I don't know. He's very angry with me for coming to San Francisco."

"And how do you feel?"

"I really don't know. Not yet."

"I'm sorry. I shouldn't have asked the question. But I could give him fair warning. I'm going to give him a run for his money. Excuse the cliché!"

She was so silent that he added quickly. "That is, if you'll let me, Tracy."

"Haven't you a girl somewhere in your background?"

He shook his head. "I'll admit there's been one, but she decided she didn't want to wait until I finished school, and so that's been over for a long time. I worked too long hours and hadn't enough money to be of much interest to anyone, I'm afraid."

Tracy looked skeptical. Why wouldn't anyone find him attractive? He danced well, wore his clothes well, was a good conversationalist. But then, maybe others might not like books!

"Do you like sukiyaki?" Miles asked abruptly.

She wrinkled her nose. "Oh, I know what you mean. I've never been to Yomato's Sukiyaki, if that's what you're thinking about."

"Then how about dinner with me there on Saturday night?"

"All right. That sounds like fun. I want

76

to see Fisherman's Wharf, too, in the sunshine, and maybe go aboard one of the old vessels, if it's possible."

"Of course it's possible. And if you'd like to go sailing some Sunday afternoon, I can arrange that, too. I have an eighth interest in a little ketch, along with some of my buddies of high school days. We just got her out of dry-dock last weekend, but she'll be ready to go in another few days."

"I'd like that, too," she said softly. She could remember one summer when she'd worked at the shop long ago. She'd gone sailing on the Bay with her aunt and uncle one weekend, and she'd always think of it whenever she saw sails scudding over blue water.

"It's getting late! It's after one-thirty!" she said. Aunt Ellen would probably be waiting up for her. And she really hadn't planned on staying out so long.

"I'm sorry." Miles rose abruptly. "Gee! I forgot all about time. It's going to be fun to show you about San Francisco and its environs! I'll get out my guide books and my maps and we'll do it up brown!"

They were still chatting away about all

the places to go, things to see and do and strange, foreign foods they must taste, when they pulled up in front of the house on Marine Drive.

"So this is where you live! Gee! I've always admired these big houses, and especially this one."

He helped her out of the car and took her to the front door, taking her key and opening it for her. He stepped inside the lighted hall for a moment.

"It was lots of fun, Miles."

"It certainly was a big evening for me," he said. "I hope I've not kept you up too late. I won't do that again on a working day," he promised.

"Good night, Miles. See you tomorrow morning."

She closed the big front door after him, turned the night lock and, going down the little hall to the den, looked for her Aunt Ellen. She expected to find her reading in her favorite chair. No Aunt Ellen!

The room was dark. And so, turning out the lamps in the living room, Tracy went up the stairs to her room. Seeing a light under her aunt's door, she tapped lightly on it.

"Come in, dear. I just crawled into bed to read a bit longer. Did you have a good time?"

"Oh, yes. Were you worried about the hour, Aunt Ellen? I'm sorry we stayed out so late. We went dancing, and also to the Top O' The Mark, after the show."

"Of course I wasn't worried about my niece! I understand distances and how long it takes to get service and how the hours fly by unnoticed when you're having a good time. I'm so glad that you had fun. It may help to make up a bit for the dreary time you've had these past two weeks."

"That's funny. You know, it's not seemed the least bit dreary, though I have worked hard."

"Of course you've worked too hard. I plan to speak to Mr. Kennedy about it."

"No! Please don't, Aunt Ellen. You'll only make him more eager to get me out of there. He thinks he'll kill me with dull work, but I've fooled him. I'm very interested in this juvenile bookshop, and I think I'll stay a long, long time."

She brushed a quick goodnight kiss on her aunt's cheek and went on to her room. If Mr. Blair Kennedy thinks he can discourage me with hard work, he just doesn't know me!

And besides that, there's Miles Stewart now.

7

ARRIVING a few minutes early at the shop the next morning, Tracy realized that for the first time since she'd started work she did not know what her day's assignment would be. Removing her hat and gloves and her suit jacket, she put them in a small cloak closet in the inner storage room.

Going to the juvenile book room, she stood for a few minutes admiring the result of her last three days' labor. She would ask for two small tables and a few youth-size chairs for the room, to add to its charm. She had begun to hope that Mr. Kennedy would turn it over to her, for she had ideas about some of the lists she could make up for parents and relatives hunting books for small fry.

On the way downtown, she had thought of getting some magazines, such as the *Horn Book, Children's Activities, Highlights, Jack and Jill* and others, to spread out on some of the low tables. And there were some clever ceramic vases of juvenile figures, filled with trailing plants and vines. A few large stuffed animals and other toys scattered about on bookshelves —but not for sale—would help build atmosphere.

Mr. Kennedy was in his office, busy at the telephone. She stopped at the desk in the new room and, looking through the memo pad, discovered there were two telephone numbers to be called today.

The shop would open in another twenty minutes, and she looked about the main salesroom to see if there were some things that she could be doing. She checked the display table, noting that several new books had been set up yesterday. The list of the top ten had been posted on the small bulletin board nearby, and the review pages of the *Chronicle*, the *Chicago Daily News* and the *Times* were also displayed. She was delighted to see that each of the new books mentioned was among those on the table.

"Ready, Miss Allen?" called Mr. Kennedy from his office door.

"Yes. Just waiting until you were

through at the telephone. What would you like me to do this morning?"

"I feel you've been here long enough to be a little oriented, so you can handle customers this morning. I have some business away from the shop for two or three hours. We've been offered a library, and I'd like to make a bid so that we may not have to compete. Do you feel up to the store?"

"Oh, yes. I'll be glad to sell books or do anything else you wish me to."

"Mr. Stewart went by the post office this morning to pick up some insured material. He'll be a little late, so will you please take all calls? Have them call me back later, so you won't have to take messages."

"Yes, sir. I'll do that, Mr. Kennedy."

"And by the way, the juvenile shop looks very good. You did a nice job, Miss Allen."

"Thank you. I enjoyed it." She was not prepared to say more; it wasn't the time yet to offer any of her ideas. This was the first really kind word he'd spoken to her during the two weeks that she'd been there, excepting when Aunt Ellen had come down one day and he'd said he thought her niece could fit into their staff all right.

"Don't underestimate her ability, Mr. Kennedy. She's a real book lover and knows how to handle customers, too." Tracy had overheard her aunt's earnest words as she passed the private office.

There were always new books to be unpacked, orders to fill and customers to please. It was a little after nine-thirty when the first customer came in. He was a small wizened old man, neatly dressed and carrying a cane.

"I want a copy of *Bonanza Inn*," he said in a trembling tone. "Right good book. One of my friends was readin' me some of it last night. Story about Old San Francisco when I was young, and then some."

"Would you like to sit down? Come right over here by our fireplace and have a chair. I'll see if we have a copy."

In the old days the fireplace had been fed big fat fir logs, but it got to be too much care when business picked up, and so electric logs had replaced the wood. It now sent up a rosy glow, and a nearby mellow pine table and big armchairs gave the corner a cozy lived-in look.

"Don't mind if I do sit a spell, Sister. It's a mite cold outside. I'll just fill my pipe, if it's all right with you."

"Certainly." She placed the canister of Bond Street Mixture beside him, and handed him the morning paper.

Bonanza Inn. She remembered reading it the year it was given to her father. That had been about five years ago, after a visit from her Uncle Stanley.

She went to the side of the room where she knew the books about San Francisco were kept. In her free moments she had studied the shelves so that she could better know the wares. The San Francisco and California collections had always entranced her. Even as a child, she had pulled books down and sampled them, to her uncle's delight.

I must read this book again, she thought as she took down a copy. There were only a few left in stock, she noted. The copyright date was 1945. *Bonanza Inn* was the story of the fabulous Palace Hotel, from its building until the theatrical ending, the last final lick of fire in 1906 which had destroyed the defiant flag, flying so high above the ruined city.

The Palace was the history of San Francisco from thirty short years after its beginnings until the great earthquake. Tracy had recognized many of the names, the streets, and the guests of the huge hotel which, in its beauteous heyday, covered four city blocks.

"Yes, sir," said the old man, as he held out his hand for the book when Tracy brought it up for him to see. "Yes, sir, it sure reminds me of many a gay evening in the old place. I was a gay blade in those days. Bricklayer by day, and a dandy by night. My father helped build the Palace, miss, and I brung his lunch to him many a day. He used to let me stand beside him and taught me how to lay bricks myself, though I was only a grasshopper."

Taking the book, he thumbed through it, and triumphantly showed her some of the pictures of places he remembered: the inner court where carriages used to come inside to deliver their passengers, and the Grand Court later designed from it. The famous theatre and opera stars, the great names in early American history, the royal families of note who had visited the hotel, all seemed of great interest to the man absorbed in its pages. He had not offered to return it to Tracy to be wrapped, but sat on and on in the wing chair, reading and turning its pages.

Tracy, amused at his wonderful interest, began waiting on other customers. Presently she came back and offered him a cup of coffee from her thermos.

He smiled gratefully. "Thankee, miss! A little drap 'bout this time does taste good." Before her startled eyes, he took a small flask from his hip pocket and poured a few amber drops into it. "Some for you?" he asked, offering it.

"Oh, no, thank you." She sipped her own coffee, wondering what was keeping Miles, and hoping to get Mr. Ralston out of there before Mr. Kennedy returned.

"I must be on my way," he said finally, half an hour after the coffee break. "Just wrap it up for me, miss, and if you've got any more books you think I'd like, let me know."

"Why don't you drop in again soon? There is a whole shelf of books over here you may enjoy." She drew him to the San Francisco collection.

His beady eyes brightened. "Never was much of a reader till lately, but it's 'bout all I can do now. I make the rounds down on Fisherman's Wharf about two days a week, and then I sit in the parks some and enjoy looking out over the Bay. Here's my card, miss. I live at the New Grand."

"I'll drop you a note if I don't hear from you soon."

The sale finally completed, she laid his card in a small inner drawer. Maybe she had made a new customer for the shop! He was carrying a large roll of bills, she had noted when he paid for the book.

Miles Stewart came in, carrying a box of books, and together they unwrapped them. They were heavily padded, and she could see that they were valuable.

"Shipped over from London for a special customer, someone by the name of Sutton, out on Russian Hill," said Miles.

"Aren't they beautiful?" Tracy asked, holding up one of the large volumes. It had been published in 1870; the handsome binding and the fine printing were a joy to see.

There was a history of Windsor Castle, with beautiful tipped-in illustrations. Tracy scanned it rather hastily. "Gee! It would be wonderful to have all the lovely books one wanted, but of course I have them vicariously, as they pass through my hands!"

"Here's another to drool over!" Miles handed her the last one from the box. It was the secret diaries of the Black Prince. "This should make interesting reading," he added.

"There's a whole set of books about the Black Prince in the University Library. One of them contains the financial records over a long period of time. I'm dying to get into the set and do a research paper on him."

"Why not?"

"Time. It would take years. But wouldn't it be a hobby?"

"Only if you cared that much about it. I'd rather go in for collecting San Francisco books. I made a small start," said Miles proudly.

"Book collectors! You should see my uncle's private collections. Actually, they should be moved out of the house."

"Into a fireproof library, of course; but don't tell me his own isn't fireproof."

"Yes, it is," she agreed. "But I'm thinking of people who would relish using the collections."

The telephone rang, and she moved to answer it.

It was one of the assistant librarians of the city schools. She was calling to find out if the list of books she had ordered last month had arrived. After securing the answer from Miles, Tracy assured her that they were expecting it this week.

"I wanted to ask you about the possibility of getting tickets for the Newberry and Caldecott Dinner during American Library Week," Tracy asked the librarian.

"It's still possible, I believe, although there are only a few left." She gave Tracy a number to call.

"Aunt Ellen's taking me," Tracy told Miles after she hung up the receiver. "Incidentally, there's a Library Science course beginning the first week in July, and I'm signing so I'll be able to audit some of the sections."

"Wonderful! That is, if the slave driver will let you off!"

"Oh, dear! But Aunt Ellen has mentioned it to him, I'm sure. Of course, if there's not time, I won't try to go. But there are to be some excellent speakers, some authors and publishers from New York, librarians from Detroit and Cleveland who are on the Children's Book Council."

"All good things, too, of course. I think you're clever to go in strong for the juvenile line. It's a staple market."

"Children's books are always popular, and they're much more permanent than some of the adult material."

"Will you call Mrs. Sutton, and tell her the books she ordered are in from London?" asked Miles.

The call finished, Tracy found other sales to be made to newly arriving customers. There were more coming in now, some to browse and some briskly to state their needs, pay and leave with the books. Just before noon a smart-looking little old woman bustled in and, coming straight to Tracy, addressed her in an excited tone.

"I was told you have copies of the old book, *Bonanza Inn*, young lady. I want one. Mr. Ralston just showed me his copy, and I can't wait to get one of my own. I used to eat dinner at the Palace with my father and mother on nice Spring Sundays, usually on Easter Sunday. I can remember it yet. We'd be all dressed up and go in to see the fine furnishings in the public reception room and the famous people. Nothing like the Palace, miss."

"We've other books, too, about early San Francisco," Tracy said, leading her over to the special shelves.

"One only today. I get my Social Security check next week and maybe I'll get another one then, miss. My eyes aren't so good, but I like to read."

After she'd gone, Tracy told Miles about little old Mr. Ralston.

"Maybe you're going to develop a whole new clientele," he said.

"It'll keep them happy for weeks, reading those books."

"Give them something to talk about, too. Time for lunch, Tracy. Why don't you go first, and I'll keep shop?"

She agreed and, before leaving, took a quick glance at the sales records for the morning. She had done rather well.

There were an impressive number of sales slips. She went next door to the coffee shop for a salad and a glass of milk. By now she had begun to recognize a few of the girls who worked in shops or offices nearby.

There was an importer's shop down the street in the next block, and Iris Langdon, one of the girls who worked there, had met her one day at lunch when they shared the same small table.

Iris was tall and blonde and rather tired-looking. She motioned for Tracy to join her, and they chatted away while waiting for their salads.

"Are you interested in Venetian glass?" Iris asked.

"Only in passing. Did you get something in that's extra nice?"

"Very nice. In fact, some exquisite pieces came in yesterday. Drop in if you've time."

"Maybe tomorrow. Today Mr. Kennedy is gone, and so we're pretty busy at the shop."

"Is Mr. Kennedy married?" Iris asked.

"I don't know," answered Tracy. "Now, really, isn't that odd? I've never heard him mention a family, and I've not asked Mr. Stewart."

"Of course Mr. Stewart's not!" laughed Iris. "He's very interested in you, Tracy. I can tell."

"You can?" Tracy asked in surprise.

"Yes, indeed. I saw you dancing last night. You looked wonderful together. And Miles didn't look around once. We used to be pretty good friends, too," she added reproachfully. "Oh, not serious, of course, but we did take our coffee breaks together last winter sometimes."

"Gee! I'm sorry! I didn't know that."

Iris laughed and said in a friendly tone, "It was absolutely nothing. You see I'm engaged. Maybe before Christmas, we'll get married and have a Hawaiian honeymoon. I'll introduce Bill to you sometime when he comes into the shop and we come over here at the same time. He's a young architect. Works in the block just beyond this on Market Street in an old office building. A small firm, but a fairly good one."

"Sounds very interesting, Iris."

"Maybe the four of us can go out together sometime."

"That should be fun." Tracy had decided her new acquaintance was someone she would enjoy knowing better. She had been a little lonely since coming to San Francisco; she missed her family and the girls of her circle back home.

"Bill's already met Miles, and they seemed to like each other. Maybe we could go down to Half-Moon Bay some Sunday; take a picnic lunch or something."

Tracy nodded. "Sounds like fun. You find out about it, and I'll ask Miles." Picnics were always fun.

She longed to stretch out on the sand, to go surf bathing, to relax. Which reminded her she had to get back to the shop and to work. They made a tentative date for the next day at lunch. "We can get away from here, go farther down to a little shop off Union Square."

"Or to Blum's, although that's usually too crowded."

"Why don't you drop by the Book Nook at twelve?" asked Tracy.

Iris agreed, and Tracy went back to her work feeling the warmth that a girl knows when she has a new friend.

8

IT seemed incredible that they could cover so much ground, eat at so many different places, see so many strange and interesting sights as Tracy and Miles managed to the next two weeks.

In the shop they did not discuss any of their adventures, and Mr. Kennedy was unaware that they were going out almost every evening together, and had spent most of Saturday and Sunday together, each of the two weekends after their first date.

It was not that they were being particularly secretive about it, but they had made a pact that they'd not let pleasure interfere with business in the shop.

On Thursday evening, after she'd stayed the required time at the office, Miles took her to Omar Khayyam's, the famed Armenian eating place. Here, Tracy renewed acquaintance with the *maitre*, Bart, and here once more she enjoyed the paintings of the Rubaiyat, the major motif

96

on the walls. It was a pleasant room, and they chose Shish Kebab and Yaprak Sarma. More than pleasantly stuffed, she regretted the rich honey cake they ate for dessert, even as she recalled her uncle's delight in the concoction.

After dinner, although it was still early, they didn't go to a show, but went for a drive instead. Miles took her up Telegraph Hill which provided a sweeping panorama view of the Bay. Thence they drove through Golden Gate Park.

They passed Coit Tower and stopped for a time at Fisherman's Wharf; getting out of the car and walking among the crowds still patronizing the fascinating shops and eating places along the sidewalks. Tracy bought two little butterfly pins from the gift shop at Tarantino's, two Spanish gold pins made in Toledo and identified by the tiny black dots along the gold lines in the design. They passed Fisherman's Grotto, Di Maggio's, the Oyster Loaf, and finally the Tadich Grill, over one hundred years old.

"Think of the millions of people who've walked these same boards and watched the lights and fishing boats moored in this small harbor," Tracy said, as they stood at the rail watching a deep sea boat unloading its catch.

Every evening proved to be holiday-like as Tracy and Miles continued dining and dancing at various places she had heard mentioned and several where she had been taken as a child.

Amelio's, Del Vecchio's, El Jardin, with such good Italian food! Mustaccioli, veal scaloppini and chicken sauté, fine wines and broiled squab a la crapaudine were among the house specialties. They avoided the more modern pizza places, preferring the cuisine of Julius Castle on Greenwich Street, high on Telegraph Hill, which had endeared itself to world visitors as well as home folks.

"Oh, dear! I can't eat at another foreign place for a month," Tracy sighed as she stayed at home one night to have dinner with her aunt. "I'll bet I've gained five pounds! I won't be able to wear my new dresses!"

"But you've danced away the extra," laughed her aunt.

They were sitting in the living room waiting for Lucy to announce dinner.

"Did you find your letter on the hall table?"

"Oh, no! I forgot to look for mail." It was Mattie's day off, and of course the mail was always left downstairs in the entry. Goes to show you how little I've thought of Bob lately, Tracy realized as she got up to go look for the letter.

She could tell it was from Bob from the inflection her aunt had used. It was addressed in his large, bold writing, and she had a sinking feeling as she tore it open. She sat down in a hall chair to read it. Last week she had written him that she was going out occasionally with Miles Stewart, and that she hoped that he would find someone interesting to go around with during summer session.

This was the first letter she'd had since her airmail had left, and though she recalled writing it, she had not given it very much thought. Her days were so filled with work, her evenings with Miles Stewart, that there was little time to think.

"So you have found someone to show you the interesting sights of San Francisco and its environs," wrote Bob. "Just as I thought! Be honest, please, Tracy. We can

99

be nothing less than that with one another. I must say I'm disappointed that you should find someone so quickly. However, I've not taken anyone else out and am not planning to. When are you coming home? It's beastly warm here, and the classes are boring. If you had encouraged me, I'd have flown down last weekend, but after your last letter, I felt deflated."

Poor Bob! Contrite, Tracy wished that she'd waited a week or so before writing him about Miles. She didn't feel any emotion because he'd not come down last weekend. A little quiver of dismay shot through her. What if he had come down? She had accepted the invitation Miles had extended. This next weekend, she and Iris and her fiancée and Miles were planning on going to Half-Moon Bay for a picnic on Sunday morning.

She put the letter into a pocket and went back to join her aunt, just as Lucy called dinner.

It was nice to eat "woman" food once more, she thought, as she touched her fork to the flaky chicken pie. A molded green lime salad with avocado and pear, the tiny green peas and new potatoes were most appetizing. She had turned down an invitation to dine at the St. Francis tonight.

"Miles, I must go Dutch if we eat out any more this month. I've cost you a fortune these past two weeks. I can read a menu, too, you know, and I note some of the prices, plus the tips!"

"Don't worry about it; we'll make it up later on hamburgers and crab louies!"

"Nevertheless, it's not fair to you. Besides, I owe it to Aunt Ellen to spend two nights a week home with her."

It was true that her aunt had begun again to seem quite worried, after having relaxed a bit when she first arrived.

After dinner they went into the den, where Aunt Ellen indicated she wished to talk a little about business.

They seated themselves, and Ellen Taylor took some papers from the desk and, glancing at them, said, "Dear, I simply cannot understand why we should not be making more profit at the shop."

"Aren't you doing all right now, Aunt Ellen?"

The older woman shook her head. "Of course Mr. Kennedy indicated long ago that we were losing a little money, but I felt that it would clear up. I still see the bills—some of them—although we do have a part-time accountant who goes over all the statements and pays all the bills. This is just so much mumbo-jumbo to me."

"I'm sure that it would be. Did Uncle Stanley indicate that he was having trouble making profit?"

"No, quite the opposite. We were doing very well just before he became ill. While he was hospitalized, I admit that things probably got a bit out of hand; but he had hired Mr. Kennedy before that and felt that the business was in good hands."

"And there's no profit at present?"

"On the contrary, we seem to be taking a little loss each month."

"I'd suggest that you have a meeting between yourself, Mr. Kennedy and the accountant."

"That's a good idea, Tracy. In the meantime, would it trouble you too much to look over some of these?" Her aunt extended a handful of papers.

Knowing that she could help slightly by recognizing some of the transactions, Tracy took them. They seemed to be invoices, orders and some bills for the new furnishings for the juvenile room. She was surprised at the cost of the tables and chairs, and wondered now at her temerity for suggesting them. She recognized the bill from the London firm for the *History of Windsor Castle* and the other books that she and Miles had examined one morning.

There were no records of sales of any of the rare books that she believed were being sold at the shop.

"How much do you get for a book like that?" she asked, after explaining the binding and print of the English books.

"They vary. Sometimes several hundred dollars. It depends on how rare they are. We have furnished books to the Sutro Library and to the historical libraries of several states for years at varying prices. Come to think of it, I believe our rare book sales seem to have been slipping lately." Aunt Ellen chewed reflectively on the tip of her pen. "Perhaps I should ask for all the records to be shown at our meeting."

"Maybe you should have a talk with just the accountant first, Aunt Ellen. It sounds horrid to accuse Mr. Kennedy of falsifying the records, unless you know that sales are being made."

"Of course, dear. I know that your uncle trusted him to carry on the business, and I shall go along. It does take time to get back on level ground, of course. How is the tea for next week coming along?"

"Just fine. Everything's under control. We'll have some well known authors signing books, including several from this area. Mr. Lee has agreed to come from one till two; Mrs. Genevieve Foster, here for the Library Science Course, will sign several of her books, and then we have Mr. McCloskey speaking at three."

"Invitations all out?"

"Every one of them, and we've had acceptances, too, in every mail. The St. Francis is sending over the tea and petit fours, and I'm getting the florist to do the flowers."

"Sounds lovely. And how are your classes coming along—when you manage to slip away?"

"Oh, I've only attended two sessions, but they were helpful, and Sister Mary Alma has kept some of the duplicate material, book lists and such, for us. It helps to give us some idea of what the schools are buying and what they're looking for."

"Just as Uncle Stanley always said, 'Smart little girl!' I'm so glad that you came. Is that young man of yours back home getting anxious?"

"He didn't much like the fact that I've been going out with Miles Stewart," admitted Tracy.

"You will have to make a decision. I like Miles Stewart, honey. He's a man's man, yet he certainly has a cultured air."

"Bob would certainly howl at that description. He thinks the whole world turns on a football."

"And you don't?" rather sharply.

"And I don't," agreed Tracy softly. "And that's not a very good basis for a marriage, is it, Auntie Ellen?" She leaned over and kissed the soft cheek. "I have some home work to do, so I'll run along upstairs."

"And what may you be doing—something for the shop?"

"Yes, I'm making out a list of books for the ten-year-old group. I brought the *Horn*

Book and several other juvenile columns home."

"Very well, dear. Don't work too late."

Tracy walked upstairs slowly. Something clicked in her mind.

There was something about the rare books situation that kept nagging insistently. She paused at the top step. Yesterday she had been back in the small anteroom where she had waited for Mr. Kennedy on that very first morning. A whole shelf of books that had been there that morning was no longer there. Where were they? Had they been put into the vaults, as Mr. Kennedy had indicated they would be? Maybe they had been sold.

Why not? But if they had been sold, why hadn't there been a record of them?

9

TRACY was uncertain of the day when she began actually to suspect that Blair Kennedy was carrying on a private enterprise of his own, using the Book Nook for its reputation and convenience. Frequently she had approached customers who asked only to see Mr. Kennedy. Even that did not seem unusual, for both she and Miles Stewart seemed to have developed their own particular fans or clientele.

Word seemed to have gotten around early in the summer that she was an authority on children's books, and so daily the demand for her suggestions, her lists and her own selections for gifts seemed to be increasing.

She therefore thought nothing of the fact that Mr. Kennedy seemed to get the wealthier, slightly eccentric, real dyed-in-the-wool bookworms until one day about the middle of July when a smartly-appearing young lady insisted on seeing only Mr. Kennedy and would not leave any message.

"I'll call later, my dear," she said to Tracy.

"Fine. Mr. Kennedy will probably be back about four. He is at Stanford today, giving a lecture to an English Conference on Literature."

"Thank you. I'll call again."

"And who shall I say called?"

"Oh, that's all right. I'll take care of it." The young lady turned and walked with a brisk step from the salesroom.

Later in the day, just before closing time, she came in again, wearing the same smart tweed suit and a small fur stole, a dark blue hat, and carrying an alligator bag which matched her high-heeled pumps.

As the door to his private office closed, Kennedy's voice asked, "Were you able to get it, Myrna?"

"Oh, yes, of course."

A few minutes later when Tracy picked up the phone to call home to tell her aunt that she was going to a show that night with Miles, she overheard Kennedy on the line.

"Yes, Dr. Sloan, I do have it. A very fine volume, just the one you hoped for."

"From the Atterbury collection?"

"None other."

"And the price?"

"I'll have to discuss it with you. It's valuable."

Afraid to put down the receiver for fear that Mr. Kennedy would know she'd been listening—which of course, she shouldn't have done, she thought contritely—Tracy heard them make an appointment for the following day in Mr. Sloan's office downtown.

She had risen and seemed to be working about the desk in front of the phone, but replaced it the second she heard the other click.

What book had he been able to get from the Atterbury Collection? And where was that particular collection?

She dared not check on it at present. She had become familiar with the names of many of the fine private collectors in the immediate area of San Francisco, and didn't recall anyone by the name of Atterbury. Of course it could be from any section, even from the East.

Kennedy had said it was very valuable.

Remembering she had planned to see if the anteroom which housed the more valuable rare books en route to the vaults was being kept locked these days, she tried the door in passing.

It was locked. Glancing inside the glass of the door, she noted that the shelves which she had seen empty a few days ago were once more occupied. She busied herself about the balcony for a few minutes, straightening rows of mysteries, adventure tales and romances. Here a few customers would sink down on the sofas and read for a few minutes, trying to decide on a selection.

Zane Grey, B. M. Bower, McCutcheon, all favorite authors of her youth, had given way to the moderns, although there were still a few demands for the older ones.

She emptied the flowers from the vase, washed it in the lavatory in the next room. Suddenly she realized that the girl and Kennedy were leaving. He checked the lights in the salesroom and locked the front door after them.

They didn't know that I'm still here! she thought.

A sharp stab of guilt struck her. *Maybe I was deliberately quiet so they would think I'd gone. There's not a chance to see the inside of the anteroom unless he's left the office door unlocked, so that I can get the key.*

His private office opened off the main office, and sometimes the latter was left open in case he or Miles should be working. Just inside a small closet was a board of keys, with the labels above them.

She waited a few minutes longer, not wanting Miles to know that she suspected anything, nor that she might be snooping. Then she went down the short flight of the balcony steps and over to the main office.

The door opened! *So far I'm lucky,* she thought.

There's really no reason I shouldn't know more about the rare books. It's odd that I'm never asked about any of them, except by newcomers to the shop. And then I am expected to refer them to Mr. Kennedy.

If Miles comes in and discovers me in the anteroom, she thought, as she entered and turned on the lights, *I'll simply tell him that I'm studying up for my job.*

There's no need for me to avoid this room; after all, I'm part of the staff!

A small room, it was about twelve feet by fourteen, and there were four large glass cases displaying several local authors' first editions and their autographs. Two or three photographs graced each of the cases, each picture inscribed to Stanley Taylor, or to both him and his wife, or to the "Book Nook."

Among the volumes displayed were several published earlier than 1940: *The California Earthquake of 1906*, by David Starr Jordan; *Ralston's Ring*, by George Lyman; *The Big Bonanza*, by Glassock; *Oscar Wilde Discovers America: 1882*, by Lloyd Lewis and Henry J. Smith.

The rare books that were worth from fifty to several hundred dollars were the ones she was really interested in checking on.

She had glanced at some of the catalogues on the desk, and now she went directly to the shelf she had noticed her first day in the shop. There were no prices marked on the fly leaves, of course. That would be too obvious.

The Secret Diary of A Southern

General, a large book with handsome covers in the middle of the shelf, caught her eye. Taking it down and leafing tenderly through it, she was so caught up in the passages which met her eye that she could scarcely put it back. There was a description of a meeting of the General with General Tarleton who had been quartered at Carter's Grove in Virginia. By the time she had replaced the book, she realized that here was a little-known story published some fifty years after the Revolution, and containing letters and the journal of a man who had been a traitor to his country.

She picked up other books: one on rare designs of early American glass. It was a book published in England in the early Nineteenth Century, reproducing some of the earliest designs of European artists who had sold their patterns to American industry. She noted it stressed Sandwich Glass, greatly prized in New England. But of course some had found its way West, too; she recalled one or two plates owned by her mother, who had received them from her grandmother.

Two folios were there, and she regretted

their being left out in this room. One was on the Boer War. One was an English translation of a Russian book.

After taking down a few titles in a little notebook, which she slipped into her tote bag, Tracy turned out the light and locked the door, replacing the key in the main office.

Tomorrow afternoon at three there would be another tea.

The first one had been quite a triumph. Aunt Ellen had come, and she had met with some of their old friends. All had expressed their delight with the resumption of the custom of tea at the Book Nook on Wednesday afternoons. Aunt Ellen had agreed to have the teas one day a week.

"It really makes them more important, and I like having them on Wednesday. For if the girls go shopping on Thursday, perhaps it's as well not to mix the two," Ellen had sighed that evening.

"It was a major success," Tracy added, "having the three authors who were here for Library Week."

Tracy sat down by the fireplace in the corner of the main salesroom, and mulled over the ideas which had been racing through her mind.

She planned to examine the vault's contents sometime. It really was somewhat surprising that she had not seen them already. After all, she presumed most employees who were members of the family which owned the shop would have been allowed to go through the whole plant by now. Odd that she'd not been sent down to place books there. There had been no further reference by Mr. Kennedy to the vaults since that first apology which he had made about the anteroom being left unlocked.

Tracy had seen the vault two or possibly three times when she was a child, and been fascinated with the lock on the inner door, after one once got through heavy steel doors. Going with her uncle when she was ten, she had imagined all kinds of things, from dragons to jewels, lurked in the inner recesses.

He had turned on a light and, to her dismay, she saw that after all a vault was really only a room. All that fuss over some more shelves, very like the ones upstairs in the small room next to the main office!

"What do you keep in here, Uncle Stanley?"

"Valuable books, dear. They won't burn here if the place gets on fire. The little safe holds some very important papers, a small reserve of cash, and two important books which I hope to sell to the Chicago Public Library next year. On these shelves," he swept his arm around the small room, "have stood some of the most fascinating books in the history of mankind."

"But what makes them valuable, Uncle Stanley? I thought most books could be bought for a few dollars, or even a few cents."

Then followed her first lesson on rare books and book collecting.

It was not to be her last, however; for every time she came back on visits, Stanley would show her some new book he had been able to purchase. She came to know a great deal about some of the fine presses, some of the famous illustrators, and had met some European as well as American authors and publishers through the years.

"All of which adds up most impressively," her uncle had said one time about two years ago. "You can go to work for

116

me when you're through school, dear. I'd consider you a valuable addition to my staff."

His half-forgotten words returned with a rush to her now. She had neglected her study of old books lately. Not the past two months, of course, for she was steeping herself once more in it. She remembered how Bob had kidded her about being so bookish.

It was one of their first disagreements. "But I like being bookish," she objected. "It's a way of life. You know, 'There's an experience for every book, and a book for every great experience!'" she loosely quoted one of her favorite lecturers.

She heard a car door slam outside in the small court.

That would be Miles coming back, probably for his glasses. She noticed them on his desk. He couldn't go to the show without them.

But it was the part-time janitor who came in about this time. She rose and, picking up Miles' glasses, put on her hat and left the shop.

As she stepped into the bright, warm sunlight, she breathed deeply. Out here in the salt breeze off the Bay, it seemed silly to think that anything of a nefarious nature was going on inside the shop she had just left.

Yet who was Blair Kennedy? Where had he come from? What were his references? She knew nothing about his training, nor of his former experience. But it's silly of me to think of these things. Her Uncle Stanley had been a shrewd businessman, she presumed. Her footsteps faltered. Had he been really? Did they all take much for granted? This shop had probably been part of his father's property which he'd inherited. In the old days a young man usually resumed or continued the work of his father, but Uncle Stanley's father had been in shipping.

Had Stanley been given the shop to play around with, after he had expressed no desire to go into the field of his father's work?

The bookshop itself was just a bit over fifty-two years old; it must have been built soon after the new structures began going up the year following the earthquake. Planned on a rather luxurious scale, it occupied a long lot, bounding the court to the left, as one entered the Lane from the street. A small inn had stood at the back at one time, and the courtyard still flaunted a statue and a flowing fountain.

Around the base of the statue, someone had planted perennials and a few geraniums which the gardener replaced every spring. The red bricks of the walk were kept brushed and washed down every day by the janitor; a bit of green lawn was clipped with a small electric trimmer kept in their own storeroom.

Was it all a play place originally given to the son of well-to-do parents who hadn't been able to settle down in his father's footsteps?

Tracy shook her head. She'd always taken the Book Nook for granted. No, indeed, it could be nothing more than a good substantial business, one from which her uncle received a very good income. She couldn't settle for anything less than that.

Prosperity in a business such as this would be real, and based on good business practices, of course.

10

AT the end of her seventh week at San Francisco, Tracy flew home for the weekend. Met by her mother and the two younger girls, she felt a surge of warmth at their welcome.

It was Friday afternoon, and she was surprised that Bob was not with them.

"He had a seminar meeting this afternoon, but he'll be out about eight," explained Susan.

She had not told her sister that Bob had been seen by Tom the week before with a pretty little local teacher who was attending summer school. They were at the drive-in theatre, and Tom had reported at the breakfast table the following morning that they seemed "cozy as anything."

Susan, indignant that they should even be out together when Bob was engaged to her sister, resented the word "cozy."

She had to find out, before Tracy was told, if there had been any new men on

Tracy's horizon in San Francisco. Tracy had not written home of her dates with Miles Stewart.

"Why don't we stop in Portland for dinner, Mom?" demanded Leslie.

"As you know very well, dear, your father will be anxious to have every minute possible with Tracy, and besides, we have a barbecue supper all ready except for the steaks which your father is going to broil. You know he'll have them out, and the charcoal will be just right by the time we get home."

"I can hardly wait," said Tracy.

"You look well. Maybe a bit thinner, Tracy," observed her mother as they neared the outskirts of the city.

"I've been working a little harder than when I first went down. And late hours, too."

"Have you been dating someone?" It was typical of Susan, who had forgotten the necessity of breaking the news about Bob gently.

"I've been going out with Miles Stewart, one of the employees," replied Tracy, sounding as casual as possible.

She didn't say that a week from today,

121

she was expecting to go home with him for dinner and to spend the night with his family. They were going sailing early the next morning.

"What's Bob going to say?"

"I'm hoping that Bob has found someone else to take around while I'm gone. It must seem a long summer."

"Gee! I think you don't make sense for someone engaged! I'd have a fit if I were going steady with someone and he took another girl out; but just think about being engaged to someone who did?"

"Now, Susan! After all, Tracy has probably given this some thought."

"Evidently Bob knows, for Tom saw him with another girl last week," put in Leslie. "Don't kick my ankle, Sue!"

"No, don't kick her ankle, Sue. And for heaven's sake, don't try to save my feelings! I wrote Bob about Miles, and I don't feel the least bit sneaky. I like Miles very much."

"Oh, boy! Tell us all about him," said Leslie.

"Don't get excited! He's been nice to me and has taken me around to see some of the places I'd heard a lot about and some of the newer spots I'd not heard about. He's lived close by—over at Mill Valley—all of his life, so he knows San Francisco."

Before they'd driven much farther, the rest of them knew quite a lot about Miles, she realized suddenly with chagrin. For someone not especially interested in a young man, she really did know a lot about him, and had let them know she did.

An hour later they turned into their home drive, and took the car around to the back. They saw Mr. Allen putting the steaks on the grill. "Heard you turning in!" he called.

Wiping his hands on paper towels, he came across the velvety grass and caught up his eldest daughter in a big bear hug.

"Couldn't wait to see you, honey. How have they been treating you down there? Looking good, isn't she, Mom?"

"Wonderful!"

Everyone helped carry out the dishes and the remainder of the supper. The part-time maid had come and cleaned that afternoon and had baked the rolls left by Mrs. Allen, and which were now rising in the slanting sun over the range. She had also kept an eye on the beans, slowly baking in the drippings from the bacon slices on top of the broad pan. Apple pie and ice cream for dessert, a large green salad ready for the blue-cheese dressing, scalding coffee. And the steaks, medium rare and fit for the Allen family—which, as the son of the family said, meant they were really something.

Tom came down from a quick shower just in time to be served with the rest of them—he had been a few minutes late getting in.

As they sat around the redwood picnic table, eating and chattering away about the summer's happenings, Tracy drank in the familiar scene lovingly. How could she have left them? And why must she go away again?

For even as she sat there, she knew that when her plane left on Sunday afternoon she'd be sad at leaving the family, yet eager to get back to her work, too.

"Couldn't you stay over for the Water Carnival, Tracy? I'm going to dive again. And I think I'm going to get a ribbon this year," begged Leslie.

"And the Country Club Dance is next

Tuesday night," said Susan. "You always go, you know."

Tracy shook her head regretfully. "Not this year, I'm afraid. Aunt Ellen really does need me in the shop. I've convinced her that she doesn't need to go at all now, and so she hasn't been down except for the teas."

"Funniest bookshop I ever saw," declared Leslie. "Imagine Faining's serving tea!" she giggled, thinking of the small bookshop which catered to their local needs. "Who'd find the time to make the tea?"

"But the Book Nook is different. It's steeped in tradition, spacious, with a leisurely clientele."

"You sound just like the feature article on Uncle Stanley's shop in *Life*, two years ago."

"It really hasn't changed much, except for the absence of Uncle Stanley." Tracy didn't want to alarm them by detailing her suspicions. Dad probably wouldn't let her return if he thought there was anything questionable going on about either sales or records.

"But he *was* the shop!" exclaimed her

mother. "I can't imagine the same atmosphere at all. He was so much a part of its atmosphere, and his pleasure at waiting on customers was so apparent that he must have made many life-long friends. Tell us, Tracy, have sales gone down?"

"Of course I've not seen records for comparison, but I can't imagine their having gone down. We have a constant stream into the bookshop. Some come out of curiosity, because of course we do advertise that we are the shop featured in *Life*; and the *Digest* reprint hasn't hurt business."

Although she had written them about the teas, their popularity, and told them about the authors whom she had met, about the new juvenile room and the fact that she was making out lists for the *Chronicle's* Christmas edition, she had to go over some of the details.

"It's just fantastic!" said Sue. "Uncle Stanley would certainly be proud of you!"

"Oh, now, I've not been responsible for all of it."

"Aunt Ellen has written glowing accounts of your help, and I'm sure your ideas are worth something to that new manager," said her mother.

"We do not have very good rapport, I'm afraid."

"Tell us about him," exclaimed Sue.

"I think I'd better get ready for Bob's date. There's really not much to tell, except that he probably thinks I'm not of any more help than a lower-salaried gal would be."

"Of course, he'd find out he was wrong soon enough!" said her mother indignantly.

Tracy wasn't sure about that yet, although she did assure herself that she was more than just an average salesclerk.

She had not had a chance to check on the vaults as yet. She thought it was much too early to voice any suspicion she might feel. Wouldn't I look silly if the books are all on record as being sold, or safely in the vault being taken care of until sold?

It was good to be home. She and her mother went toward the kitchen bearing a tray loaded with dishes, followed by other members of the family, also loaded, as was the custom after their outdoor meals. They made short work of clearing up.

"Better run along and unpack your dresses," said her mother. "Sue and I can put these things into the dishwasher."

Tracy took a good long look at the living room, familiar in its details: the low green sofa, with the lamp tables and lamps at each end, the big fireplace with the Chinese vases on the mantel, the new wooden clock, with its bold golden figures on the dial and its lovely scrolled gold medallions. She admired the sage-green of the new wall-to-wall carpeting her mother had purchased in the spring, noted that the two Gainsborough chairs in their linen upholstery looked as new and fresh as the day they'd been bought.

Leslie burst through the French doors of the family room. "Gee, Sis, I've sure missed you. When are you coming back to stay?"

Tracy kissed her, and gave her a quick squeeze. "That makes me feel very good, honey."

"Gosh, it's lonesome without you. Sue's so busy this summer. Do you think I could go home—rather back—with you?"

"Well, maybe you shouldn't this

summer, because Aunt Ellen's not feeling too well. Maybe later—"

As she went up to dress for her date, Tracy thought of each member of the family separately. Her parents seemed well, and the rest of them busy and happy as usual. Of course, Leslie, like most kids her age, was at a loss to fill all the hours in a summer's day.

Summer would soon be over, though. This thought brought a sigh. What was Bob planning to do this fall? Would he continue in school, or would he play professional football?

Maybe she would find out in a short time. She began to hurry, seeing that she had only half an hour, and that Bob was usually prompt.

11

BOB was as well groomed and handsome as ever, Tracy thought. Wearing a pair of light gray flannel slacks, a white sport coat and white shoes, he looked like summer in the Williamette Valley. In San Francisco one rarely saw a man wearing white—either shoes or suit of any kind—unless he was a tourist who had not been prepared for San Francisco weather.

Tracy had brought home a sheer green dress which she had purchased for dancing in San Francisco. Though ordinarily she would have had little use for it on such a warm evening, she caught up Susan's short white coat which had been offered to her.

The two made a handsome couple as they left the house to get into Bob's new car. The fact that he had a new car surprised Tracy; she knew almost instantly that he was not planning on going to school in the fall. He would need his money for tuition and board and room—not car payments!

"Gee! It's a beauty, Bob."

"Thought maybe you'd approve! I got tired working the old one over every weekend, and it seemed that any time I really needed it, the blasted thing wouldn't run." He helped her into the cream-colored convertible.

The top was down, so she put on the white coat and they rolled down the tree-lined avenue toward the country.

"Thought you might like to go riding, and that maybe we'd drive over to Newport and go dancing at the Hi-Tide or Beach Club."

"Sounds fine! Gee, how long have you had the car?"

"About three weeks now. Didn't I write you?"

"No. Not that it matters."

He had bought it, then, before she'd written that she was going out with Miles Stewart. He must have decided early in the term that he was going to play football in the fall.

"What are your plans for September, Bob?"

"I could say they depended upon your plans," Bob said, slowing down. He drew out a cigarette and lit it. "But that really wouldn't be true, Tracy. I've thought a lot about what to do, and it always adds up to one answer. I've signed a contract for pro football for next fall. I know you want me to do what I think best—I can always come back to school. Coaches are pretty scarce, too, and I think I can always find a school job when I get ready for it."

"Quite probably, Bob. Coaching jobs are usually fairly plentiful, and as you say, you can probably find one when and if you decide that you'd like it." It was best that he try his hand at pro football for a while at least. If he didn't he would always wonder if he shouldn't have.

"Tell me how you really like working at the bookshop." He smiled at her.

"Letters are rather unsatisfactory. I have tried to indicate that I like the work, Bob; it's really much more interesting than I'd dreamed. Sometimes it's hard, too, but I'm strong and usually snap out of it."

"You look as pretty as ever. At least it agrees with you. Now tell me about this Miles Stewart."

That would be difficult. "He's been showing me the city. I'll admit I was rather lonesome until he asked me out a few times. I hope you've been enjoying the summer." It was strange, but she really did hope that he was having a good time.

"It was very dull without you. Lately I've been seeing a little of Lana Baldwin. She's a local teacher, doing some graduate work this summer."

"Oh, yes! I know her." It suddenly occurred to Tracy that she had met the girl. She was a history teacher at the high school. She was a small blonde with a vivacious personality, dressed very well and shared a small apartment a few blocks from the campus.

"You don't mind, do you, Tracy? There's not even been a kiss between us. She can't take your place, darling." Bob leaned over and kissed her on the lips.

They had not kissed when he arrived a few minutes earlier because there were too many people around. She still experienced a feeling of shyness in public, would only kiss him when they were alone.

She smiled mistily at Bob. Most girls would have considered Lana a threat.

Right now Tracy felt confused. She had never been kissed by Miles Stewart. They had always had fun, but had never really lingered in the evening when he took her home. It was usually late, and he always seemed contrite at having kept her out so long.

Strange that all of these thoughts should rush pellmell through her head at this moment.

"Have you missed me a little?" pleaded Bob.

"Of course I have! How about you, Bob?"

"You know the answer to that, Tracy. I was really pretty sore when you left for San Francisco. I didn't think it quite fair when I'd planned on seeing you; you made summer school a little more bearable. In fact, I'm pretty sure I'd not have come back if I'd dreamed you wouldn't be here. I turned down a good job just before leaving Seattle." His tone was more than slightly accusing.

She felt considerably shaken. She had been very selfish! Why hadn't it occurred to her that it really might have changed Bob's plans? "I didn't know myself that I

134

was going until that Sunday afternoon, Bob. Aunt Ellen's letter was a complete surprise to us, you know. Gee! I'm sorry about the job. Would you really have liked to stay home this summer?"

"It's just as well I came. I'll be through with the course, and not have to take that again. If I don't go into coaching, this could very well be my last appearance in a classroom!"

"Oh, don't say that! Of course you'll be back!" But would he?

Bob drove rather fast. They were passing through a forest, and the deepening shadows made the air seem cold. Tracy shivered a little, and Bob drew her closer to him.

"Honey, you must have known the minute you saw this car that I'm going to play pro football. I didn't really have to tell you that a while ago."

"Where will you go first?"

"Oh, we start training in August. Probably in San Francisco, or nearby."

"Why, that's nice!" she said.

"I was hoping that if you stayed on, we'd see each other a lot during August. Really, darling, you could name a wedding date now. As far as I'm concerned, what I'll be doing for at least two seasons is settled."

"Two?"

He nodded. "I signed for the next two. Really, it wouldn't be worthwhile to sign for just one."

"I suppose not."

"And how about the date for our wedding?"

"Don't you think it would be a good idea for you to feel free the first season, Bob? We've always thought that until you got a bit settled, it would be better to wait."

"Of course you're right—as always, honey. It would be better for you, and probably you'd have had enough of a career behind you by that time so that you'd be willing to give up your job if you wanted to come with me. Some of the wives do; some stay on jobs, or at home with the kids."

Kids. Tracy, like any girl, had thought of the children that she and Bob would some day have. They seemed a bit shadowy and indistinct in her mind tonight. Her job loomed pleasantly in her thoughts. A quick picture of the logs in the fireplace, the colorful shelves of books in the juvenile room, flashed through her mind.

"It will be fun having you down in San Francisco, Bob."

"I'll probably be there the third week of August."

"Where will you be staying?"

"I'm not sure yet, but as near the field as possible, I suppose. I was talking with the manager last week, and he said some of the fellows share an apartment, and hire a cook so they can have balanced meals."

"Sounds like you'll be in training!"

"Natch!" He squeezed her hand. "But not such strict training that I can't take my girl out dancing."

They were nearing the town of Newport now, and the new highway that had eliminated the old curves which were so hazardous allowed him to drive faster. It was dark when he drove out to the Beach Club where they had decided to go. The big neon sign denoting the drive up to the lodge was flashing, and several cars were already in the parking lot. It was almost nine by the time they had had a cool drink and began to dance.

A number of other couples were dancing, too, and the orchestra, though small, was unusually good for the Beach Club. If it weren't for the tourists, they really couldn't afford to keep an orchestra going all summer, Tracy thought, knowing that Saturday was their biggest night. She had been over on the Coast many times during her college years. It was quite the thing to drive over from Corvallis to spend the evening with one's date; however, the fog had sometimes made it very dangerous on the old, curving road which had been replaced. Her parents hadn't always approved her driving over to Newport, but now, since her engagement to Bob, they were more tolerant.

As she danced with him, Tracy wondered about Lana. Did Bob like her rather well? Or was she just someone to go around with? After all, a man with a new car needed some feminine company to enjoy it. She had brought this situation upon herself—had created the necessity of looking for another girl to share his new car.

When they returned to their small table, she realized that she hadn't felt a pang of regret about having gone to San Francisco to work in the Book Nook, even if Bob were taking out Lana Baldwin.

But what if he should fall in love with Lana? she asked herself forthrightly.

That's a chance we have to take. After all, we've been dating steadily for more than a year, and I've been wearing Bob's pin for four months or so now.

If he had money to buy a new car, he did have money to buy you a ring, said her inner voice. I had my chance, she told herself. He asked me to meet him at the jeweler's the very day that I left for San Francisco. *Yes, and if you'd really been in love with Bob, if you'd really been excited about the thought, you'd have met him there, too!*

Very well, I probably would have. What kept me from going?

Not being sure about it. And don't think about FATE! People sometimes make their own fate. She recalled reading an article in the *Digest* about this very subject. One could direct his life by using common sense and by better planning.

Bob was handsome. He asked me for a date. I dated him, and the girls in my crowd thought it rather wonderful that the football captain and such a wonderful player pinned me.

"What are you thinking about so deeply?"

"Us," she answered lightly.

"That's good." He took her near hand and held it. "I didn't think you'd been thinking much about us for the past two weeks, Tracy, for your letters became scarcer."

"We've been busier than usual in the shop," she said.

"Be truthful, honey. Haven't you been seeing more and more of that Miles Stewart? Darn it, Tracy, I am jealous of the guy."

"Not really, Bob! You don't need to be. Why, he's never even kissed me."

"He'd better not, if he doesn't want a punch in the nose."

"Oh, come now, Bob!" Tracy laughed. "You know better than to be that uncivilized. After all, I didn't think you'd mind too much. It's dreadfully lonely in a big city when you're more or less alone, and I've been used to you—and a big family, too. It makes a difference."

"Indeed it does. You may recall I tried to get you not to go. In fact, I begged you not to leave me."

"Something drove me. Maybe it's like your needing to go into pro football to see for yourself, Bob. We're two intelligent people. If I'd not gone, I'd always have felt guilty about not helping Aunt Ellen out."

"She could hire someone else to do that job. After all, there are probably six great colleges or Universities within telephoning distance, and they might just possibly have produced at least one graduate capable of doing what you're doing."

Tracy stared at him unbelievingly.

"You *are* jealous, Bob."

"Certainly. Jealous as the very devil. And as I said, Aunt Ellen could have found someone else."

Tracy paled. "I realize that no one's indispensable. But I like to think that I've given Aunt Ellen some kind of help that you don't find with just the ordinary sales clerk. I've helped her over some lonely evenings . . ." She broke off.

She couldn't very well say, "And I'm trying to find out what's wrong with the Book Nook." I can't tell him that I'm suspicious of the manager who has been working there for months.

"Seems to me that you were responsible for some lonely evenings for *me*," Bob said stiffly.

"We're almost quarreling, Bob."

He stared at her silently for a long moment. "So we are, and it's your fault."

12

LATER they regained their light mood and the evening finished as many of their dates had, with a ride home in the soft moonlit night. The top of the convertible was up, because it was quite cool after one o'clock. They arrived a little after two, which was very late indeed, but still time enough to go to their favorite small restaurant and have bacon and eggs and coffee.

Tom was already home, Tracy noted, seeing his car in its stall in the garage. Bob came only to the door, but he kissed her warmly on the lips after opening the front door with her latchkey. "I'll see you tomorrow night, honey. How about dinner at the Inn just outside town?"

"All right, Bob. Maybe a little after seven, though? I don't get to see much of Dad."

"Okay. And maybe we could go to the Timberline Lodge Sunday morning, and I'll take you to your plane."

"Fine, Bob." A feeling of regret came over her. She would not get to see much of the family unless she spent every moment just visiting them.

Saturday was rushed. She went grocery shopping with her mother in the morning and they stopped at her father's store.

As always, she was entranced with the hardware, the seed and garden supply room, the shining new cutlery and pots and pans which had always made it a place of delight.

"Gee, Dad! If it hadn't been books, I'd have probably been under your feet next winter."

"You can always reconsider, you know," he said. "Come over here and look at these new blenders we just got in."

"Do you have one yet, Mother? Or are you like the cobbler's children?"

"Oh, I've trained him; now he brings them home for me to try before he orders a big shipment."

"How about lunch with the old man? I'd look good going down the street with two pretty girls," her father said proudly.

"Wonderful. We'll call the kids and tell 'em," said Tracy.

"I hinted as much," said her mother. "In fact, I think Leslie was going to bicycle over to her girl friend's house for hamburgers. And you know Sue. Maybe she'll run down and join us."

They ended up by going into the Elk's Club for a very good luncheon. Sue did join them, and they formed a pretty family picture at the big round oak table where they were greeted by several businessmen out lunching.

It's fun, this small town life, thought Tracy happily. Gee, I really would miss all of this if I ever decided to give it up completely.

After lunch Tracy thanked her father, saying, "I'm so glad we got to spend that time with you, Dad, for I promised Bob I'd go out to dinner with him tonight."

"That's all right, honey. I'm glad to get a few extra minutes with you, for I know how it is. Sometimes we don't see much of Tom, and the other two are growing up fast."

The afternoon passed swiftly. "While we're here, we might as well shop for a new summer evening dress for me," Sue exclaimed. "My old one won't do for the next dance at the Country Club."

"Gee! Sounds like old times, doesn't it, Mother? You've heard that lament before. Have a new dress on me, Sue! I'd love to buy one for you."

"You must be simply rolling!"

"Oh, no! And my flight ticket was a bit expensive, you know."

"I will appreciate it, Sis, but you don't really need to."

"I can just hear that don't-you-dare-back-out tone!" laughed Tracy. "Come on; let's go into the Gown Shop."

"They're having a sale," squealed Sue. "Look!"

It was like so many other occasions when they'd shopped, the two pretty Allen girls—plus their mother, who looked quite young.

"You resisted nobly, Tracy," Sue commended her after they'd made the selection.

Susan had bought a pretty pink sheer, with silver threads shot through it, which gave her an ethereal quality. "I'll loan it to you sometime," she offered Tracy.

"Maybe we can get together on things now and then."

"Oh, no, Tracy. Really, I couldn't wear your beautiful dreamy dresses," said Sue longingly.

"We'll see," Tracy said. She made up her mind to send Sue something now and then. She could recall how it was to need an evening gown and not to have one in sight!

She dressed simply for the evening, wearing a printed dress of rosebuds on white, with a casual white sweater over her shoulders. Her black hair piled high, she was lovely, and Bob looked upon her appreciatively as he escorted her into the Inn about seven-thirty.

Several couples they'd known for years were there, too. She wondered if Bob knew they'd planned to be there. They were greeted effusively, for they were always very popular.

"Gee! It's great to see you, Tracy. Looking mighty fetching," said Dan Lindstrom. He was escorting one of her sorority sisters, Nancy Deering, who had risen and kissed Tracy heartily.

It was again like old times. They had a

large table, dined generously on fried chicken and finished with their favorite ice cream. "Of course it was a surprise!" laughed Nancy. "When Bob said you were coming, we decided to get together for a party. You're coming to my house to dance on the new family room floor before Mother has the carpet laid. Then we'll go boat riding, if anyone wants to, or out to the Club and dance until morning."

"We just couldn't let you get the idea that life's humdrum back here," said Mary Lance. "Tom said you were having a pretty good time in the big city."

"I've always liked San Francisco, but you know home looks mighty good, too."

It was a wonderful evening, she told Bob later. There had been the usual great fun with all of the friends who had gathered at Nancy's. They danced until almost eleven; then, going to the club, they continued until it closed. Going on downtown, they had scrambled eggs at the all-night café close to the theatre where they'd watched the movies through the years.

It's made me homesick, Tracy thought as she brushed her hair before getting into bed. She really was terribly sleepy, and this had not been what one would term a quiet, restful weekend at home, by any means. She would struggle through the next few days. Maybe she could fall asleep on the plane the next day and catch up on a few winks.

Bob picked her up at nine for their trip to Timberline, and she confessed she'd just as soon have slept. They rode quietly most of the way up the mountain. Mt. Hood was snowcapped, which was a bit unusual for this late in the month.

"Just for us. It's probably too slushy to ski on. The Golden Rose Tournament was held two weeks ago."

They had lunch in the restaurant at the Lodge and found they didn't have too much time to loiter before the plane left. She had called in her confirmation, so that she wouldn't have to get there much before take-off time.

But it was really mostly a morning of driving, and she wondered later if she wouldn't really have done better to eat a leisurely breakfast with her folks, rather than be rushed around with Bob.

He kissed her at the gate, holding her

close for a minute. "Oh, Bob!" she gasped. "People are looking."

"Let 'em look!" He grinned. "Gates are places to kiss people who are leaving on planes, or getting back from trips!"

"Flight Forty-Nine now loading at Gate two! Oakland, San Francisco and Los Angeles, Dallas, Phoenix!"

"Goodbye, Bob. Write me!"

"'Bye, Sweetheart." Bob was still standing there when she looked back just before entering the cabin of the plane.

They waved. It would be several weeks before she'd return home again, but he would be down in San Francisco soon.

She found her seat, next to the window, and watched the plane leave the runway. She always felt a sense of delight when a big bird rose and skimmed far above the trees and she could see the city checkered beneath them.

She thought she would go right to sleep, but found herself thinking of the hours she'd spent with Bob. She had been surprised to find that he had so deeply resented her leaving for the summer. She did feel remorseful that she had caused him to give up a job in Seattle. However, as he'd said, it had really been a good thing for him to finish the course he needed.

With a little sinking feeling of dismay, she realized that she would not see Miles nearly so often after Bob came. Actually, she supposed, she would only see him at the office.

It's not fair to Miles for me to keep on seeing him so often.

But there was no reason for Bob to be jealous. None whatsoever. Really? her conscience asked.

Very little! she thought indignantly.

Be honest with yourself. To thine own self be true. I have enjoyed Miles a lot. It has been fun to go out with him.

All right, then, face it. You like Miles. You like him very much. He has high ideals. He is considerate, practical, intelligent, and loads of fun.

Loads of fun? Well, wasn't Bob, too? On what did one base a marriage?

Bob's face should be uppermost in her mind. But when she asked herself that question: On what did one base a marriage? why should Miles' face suddenly appear in her mind?

Bob hadn't mentioned Lana Baldwin again. But Nancy Deering had. "I don't think it's the least bit serious, Tracy, but I do think you ought to come home."

"Thanks for your consideration, Nancy," she had said. "But Bob's coming down to San Francisco in August." She couldn't tell Nancy that Bob was going into pro football. It was strange that no one had mentioned it last night. If Bob had wanted them to know, it did seem as though he'd have mentioned it.

Nancy and Mary were going to work in Portland in the fall. One of the couples was being married in October. All of the rest planned to go to the wedding. Tracy and Bob had promised to attend; even though it might be a problem for Bob. It did seem that he might have mentioned his contract at that time, but he hadn't.

The stewardess served coffee and Tracy went to sleep soon afterward, napping until they landed at the airport.

To her surprise, Miles Stewart met her plane.

"I just called your Aunt Ellen and asked what time you'd get in," he said. "It's been lonesome as all get-out here. Dull as can be this weekend! If we plan just right, I'll have time to take you down the coast for dinner. How about it?"

He looked so eager that Tracy hardly had the heart to turn him down. It had been good of him to meet her. It had saved Aunt Ellen the trouble of having to get the car out and drive down when she might not feel up to it.

Miles held her hand a little longer than necessary. For a moment, when she had first spied him and he had hurried up, she'd thought he was going to kiss her. But they had both paused abruptly, and she'd thought nervously, just in time, too!

"Oh, Miles, I'm absolutely dead!" her better judgment triumphed. "I've really had quite a weekend."

"But you do have to eat somewhere. How about a crab louie or a sandwich, if you had dinner at noon?"

"Tempting me? I'll tell you what: I'd really enjoy a crabburger at Fisherman's Wharf, if you would."

"It's a deal. And I'll take you on home afterward, if you wish. But I was sort of counting on spending the evening with you."

"Not tonight, Miles, or I won't be able to get any work done tomorrow. Thank you so much for meeting me." She sounded rather formal, and contritely she added, "It made the trip just perfect!"

13

THE week following her visit home, Tracy worked very hard at the shop, staying over the supper hour two nights, thoroughly cleaning and dusting all the books in the juvenile room, making out lists and preparing herself for the inauguration of the Story Hour on Saturday morning.

She was not at all certain that Blair Kennedy approved the program, although he had agreed to try it. It was bound to interfere with business as usual, for she would not be available to sell books to customers, and probably Kennedy would need to stay in the shop.

"Think of all the trade we may induce by having the Story Hour," she had smiled at him.

"We'll see. You may have quite an idea here."

"I think the kids will enjoy dramatizing the stories, and I've planned to have the Review Committee report on some new books, which should help business."

"Sales have been good this past month," Kennedy said.

"Wonderful!" Her enthusiasm was wholehearted.

"Maybe Mr. Stewart can take over in the main salesroom, while you're busy with the kids."

They planned the program carefully. But they were not really prepared for the number of youngsters who descended upon the shop at ten the following Saturday. They seemed literally to come in droves. Ushered into the juvenile room, they sat in the chairs, overflowed them to the floor, and soon the room was packed.

Tracy began to tell the story promptly at ten o'clock, for some of the first ones had arrived at nine-thirty. She could not afford to entertain them by passing out new books, for, careful as they might be, they would damage the books so that all of them would need to be sold at a reduction.

They were surprisingly quiet before the program began. Nevertheless she thought that she must be prepared for little surprises like this and have something for them to do. Perhaps they'd plan on using certain books as samples.

Tracy told the story, "East of the Sun and West of the Moon," and from the smallest to the oldest they were entranced with it.

Perhaps because she had loved the story herself as a youngster, and perhaps because she had told it frequently as a baby-sitter to Leslie, she had almost memorized it.

After a few minutes, at the close, she suggested that they dramatize it. She had passed around a book which they signed with their ages next to their names.

While she picked the cast, two of the older girls served lemonade which she had ready for them. "All in all," Tracy said happily to her Aunt Ellen at home that night, "it proved to be highly successful. We may have to hire a hall, though! We had to turn away some of the kids who came after ten o'clock. That teaches them to be prompt, of course, and lends attraction to the program to think there wasn't room to accommodate all of them."

"You may need to use the Public Library then, dear."

Tracy nodded. "It would be quite a job to transfer all the books we want to use, though."

"Not necessarily. Miss Travers, the librarian, will arrange it for you, I'm sure. And it won't be too much trouble to take some books over there. We've done these things through the years, dear." Aunt Ellen patted her arm. "Miss Travers can help you make the selection from their own shelves. It encourages more reading, greater use of the Library, and helps business, too."

"We'll probably need to announce it at the next Story Hour, then," said Tracy. "One more Saturday like this one and I'll be willing to use the Library. I could hardly get them to leave. One little boy spilled his lemonade, too."

"That's to be expected, of course."

Tracy went upstairs to get ready for her date with Miles. This was the evening she was to go home with him to Mill Valley, and although it had been planned for some time now, she had misgivings. After all these weeks she would meet his family, and was even spending the night, because the next morning she and Miles, Iris and

158

her fiancé planned to go down the coast, to swim and to picnic before returning to San Francisco.

It had been a very busy week. Tracy and Miles had not gone out together at all. She had excused herself by telling him that she had too much to do to get ready for her program, too much to catch up with, because of the trip last Saturday when she had gone home. Miles had accepted the explanation without questioning. Still, Tracy felt a little guilty.

She could hardly say, I've suddenly decided we're seeing too much of each other, Miles.

Looking back at the past few weeks, she realized how many evenings they had spent together. It really was unfair to Miles to see that much of him and suddenly break off when Bob came to town.

She had put a few things into her overnight case: a pair of pajamas and nylon robe, slippers, bathing suit, towel and swim cap, cold cream and other cosmetics. She decided on wearing a light tweed suit and dacron sweater.

She had had two letters from Bob this

week, and she had written three; one, of course, a thank-you note on her arrival. She found that he discussed his prospective arrival in his last letter. It was all settled now where he would stay, and he knew the date he expected to get there.

August 20.

"Our team plays the All Star Team at Los Angeles. Honey, I do feel proud of being on the '49ers at last. They approached me my Junior year here at college, and when I made the All American it was practically settled as far as they were concerned. I do hope that this will meet with your approval. Of course, I can see that from your point of view the life of a faculty wife would appeal to you more than being a follower of a pro football team. Be patient with me, and perhaps I'll find myself on a campus some day to stay."

She re-read the letter just after she completed her dressing, and it bolstered her for the evening with Miles. She must be completely friendly, but she must not

160

give Miles any reason to become serious about her. So far they had simply enjoyed going about with each other. There was nothing very serious in their friendship.

Suddenly she knew that he had not been taking any other girl out. He couldn't have. I'm just trying to deceive myself, by thinking that he could possibly be going out with anyone else.

She heard his car in the drive and hurried downstairs. Mattie let him in while she was in the study saying goodbye to her aunt. She paused contritely at the door. Aunt Ellen was sitting in her big chair, and although it seemed pleasantly warm to Tracy, her aunt was wearing a rose-colored shawl over her shoulders, and her face looked pinched in the late afternoon sunlight which filtered through the blinds.

"Do you want me to leave you overnight?"

"Oh, certainly, Tracy. It just seemed a bit chilly, and Mattie brought the shawl until the logs catch on and the room gets warmer."

"Seems so odd to need a fire in the summer."

"We have a little heat almost every day

of the year, you remember. Tell Mr. Stewart hello for me."

"I'll let him tell you himself, Auntie." Stepping to the hall, she called to him. He smiled and touched her hand briefly.

He came to the door, then crossed the room and gravely shook hands with Mrs. Taylor. "I'm glad to see you. How are you?" His tall frame bent over her solicitously. "We've missed you down at the shop, Mrs. Taylor. Some of your friends were asking about you today."

"Thank you, Mr. Stewart. I may get in one day next week, but I've not been very well this summer."

"Is there anything I can do for you or get you?"

He sounds just like Dad! Tracy thought. He sounds so sincere, and he would go to any lengths to help her. An odd thought came to her. We may have an ally in Miles if we should ever need one.

As they drove along through Golden Gate Park on their way to the big bridge, she thought, I wish I could tell him about my suspicions, but I don't dare. He'd think me silly, I'm sure. No, I have to discover something more definite.

162

She felt suddenly that she must find out if Miles knew very much about the rare book business as it was practiced at the Book Nook.

"Could we possibly make one exception, Miles?"

"About what?" He smiled down at her.

"About shop talk?"

"Strictly banned. It'll cost you a quarter."

"And worth it, too! I have a question: Does the Book Nook do a good trade in rare books?"

An odd expression crossed Miles' face. "I really don't know. You could talk to Mr. Kennedy about it." He withdrew a cigarette from a pack and lit it.

Tracy felt that he was giving himself time to think about how to answer her. She felt herself stiffening, and turning cool toward him. Did he know that something was going on, and were her suspicions justified?

"I take care mainly of the new books, orders for new customers and the old steady ones. You know: mysteries, best sellers, text books. Mostly the lighter stuff, the sort you yourself handle. It's a pretty good plan. As manager, Mr. Kennedy really doesn't have time to handle the volume of sales I do. It's only natural for him to sell the few rare books and folios, the documents, et cetera. I prefer it this way myself."

"But don't you know anything about his sales?" burst from her lips.

Miles kept his eyes on the road. "Very little, I confess. I do know there are a few customers—clients, I suppose you'd call them. Sometimes he hunts for weeks before he locates a book demanded by someone. Usually they are not the customers themselves, but representatives for clients."

She took a sudden shot in the dark. "Like Myrna?" she asked.

He sent her a quick, questioning look. "Who's she?"

"I presume one of the representatives. She was in the shop some time ago. Both of you were gone. Later she came back, and I thought she was interested in rare books. I could be wrong."

"You know, Tracy, I wouldn't worry about anything except my own department if I were you. You have plenty to do with

164

your new program, and acting as advisor to young parents!"

She laughed lightly. "Oh, I manage to keep busy, Miles. It's just that Uncle Stanley always talked to me about rare books and showed me some of his finest, and I miss not knowing anything about them. I haven't dared ask Mr. Kennedy. He's so distant, you know."

Miles nodded. "Yes, he keeps everything on a formal basis; it's best that way."

"But it's not that kind of a shop. At least it didn't use to be!"

"Perhaps it's just as well that things are more formal. There's a different kind of merchandising from what there was in the old days. Customers who come in two or three times a week for tea are time killers. Perhaps they don't buy enough to pay for their tea."

"You're kidding, of course! I'll bet some of those customers gave huge orders every Christmas, and on special occasions other gifts. Many of them had standing orders for all the best sellers, and kept their own shelves open by giving books to the hospitals and schools."

"Good girl! I've always felt that there's

something special about handling books—
if one operated where there's real money.
There are a few fabulous shops about the
country where a great volume of business
is done more or less on an informal basis.
But taken by and large, no dealer can
really afford the time involved in the
hospitable practices your uncle enjoyed."

"Sometimes I think it was more for the
social prestige." Tracy sighed. "But it was
fun. Even Aunt Ellen enjoyed coming
down to the shop."

"Is she worried about the business?"
Miles asked bluntly.

"Yes."

"Have you thought about asking her to
discuss it with her attorney and seeing how
he feels about it?"

"Do you know that Aunt Ellen hasn't
seen any of the rare book records, and not
many of the others, since Uncle Stanley
died? Oh, Miles, I know I shouldn't talk
to you about all this, but I've been
worried, too."

"I'm sorry." Miles took one of her
hands. "I'm not sure just how far you can
go with this matter. If Mr. Taylor hired
Mr. Kennedy in good faith, and if the

accountant is doing what he should, then there's no reason you should worry about any of it. It's only natural that the business should fall off for a period of time after your uncle's death. But give it a leveling off period, and then everything should be all right again."

"I'm sure that's a sensible way to look at it." Tracy smiled at him gratefully. "And you won't discuss this with Mr. Kennedy?" she pleaded. "You won't let him know we've been worried?"

"I promise, of course. What do you take me for, a squealer?" He grinned at her. "And now pay me that quarter and let's forget it!"

14

MILES had a few misgivings as he drove into the new carport at home. What would a girl like Tracy Allen think of his home and his family? They were just a cut above ordinary people, he liked to think. Nothing truly distinguished about any of them; they were honest, hard-working, and always questing for an education. Witness his folks sending him to Stanford when they really couldn't afford it. Of course, he'd helped earn his way, but educating three children cost money these days!

Karen, his seventeen-year-old sister, greeted them on the narrow front porch. She was pretty, with a lovely skin and flashing brown eyes, a dark pony tail and a pretty figure encased in a striped tee shirt and Bermuda shorts.

Miles introduced them, and Tracy felt Karen's friendly scrutiny. "I just knew you'd be pretty and awfully nice," she confessed later as they went upstairs to

Tracy's room. "You know, you're the only girl that Miles has ever brought home."

"Not really?"

"Uh huh. Here's the bathroom, and here's the room you're to share with me, if you don't mind?" There were twin beds covered with flowered blue chintz, crisscrossed white curtains blowing inward with the slight summer breeze of a late afternoon. A sudden feeling of homesickness hit Tracy. It might have been one of their own bedrooms back in the Willamette Valley.

"It's fine. Looks like home! Oh, Karen, what a beautiful view!" Tracy crossed the polished oak flooring and pulled aside one of the curtains. The house sat atop a hill, overlooking a deeply forested valley. A few small redwood houses with decks such as the one immediately below her were visible at intervals among the trees.

"Isn't it pretty?" agreed Karen. "I'm crazy about this place. I've never lived anywhere else, and of course I suppose we miss something by not living in the city."

"Not at all. This is much better, Karen. Oh, San Francisco is exciting, but it's not really a place to rear a family. Not like this atmosphere, anyway. I smell barbecuing steaks!"

"Right! Dad always grabs any excuse to cook outdoors this summer. He likes to show off our new outdoors fireplace. Mom gets everything else ready, but the steaks are his province."

"Sounds just like my folks! I had barbecued steaks one week ago last night at home."

"No kidding!" Laughing, the two girls went back downstairs.

"It's a love of a house," said Tracy.

"Old, but refurbished and added on to. Mom's just making new draperies for the family room. We'll probably bring in our suppers if it gets too cool."

Going out to the deck and patio, they met the other members of the family: Mr. and Mrs. Stewart; Charles, their twenty-year-old son; and Belshazzer, an English wolf hound.

Mrs. Stewart was pretty, with dark hair and brown eyes, a slim figure and a quick smile. Her husband was tall, thin and grey-haired, with distinguished features, belying the white apron and tall chef's hat.

"Make yourself right at home, Miss

Allen. Mind if we call you Tracy?" he asked. "Somehow steaks and formality don't seem to go together very well out here on the sun deck."

"Better call it moon deck if we don't hurry and eat!" suggested Charles. "Can I carry anything out for you, Mom?"

"Yes, you can bring the wooden bowl of salad greens, and maybe Tracy will toss it with the dressing. Get it off the kitchen counter, Charles, and don't spill anything!"

"Yes, ma'am! Down, Belshazzer! Stay!"

The big white dog stopped in his tracks and went back to lie down again in the place where he had been worshipfully gazing up into the boy's face.

"Be a good dog and you can go walking with us after supper," said Miles, reaching out a hand and rubbing the dog's back. "He likes to chase squirrels and chipmunks," he added to Tracy.

"I don't blame him; so do I!"

Karen laughed. "Gee! You sound like one of the family." A red blush stained her face and she apologetically frowned at Miles, who pretended not to see her.

A few minutes later Mr. Stewart called, "Come and get 'em!"

They formed a line and were rewarded with foil-wrapped baked potatoes and sizzling steaks; each helped himself to a big kettle of green beans with bits of ham, hot garlic bread and bowls of green salad. Washed down with cups of strong black coffee, the food tasted wonderful to Tracy.

"I'll need that walk, Miles," she groaned after the last bite. "And if it's all right with you, Mrs. Stewart, I'll eat my dessert later."

"Wise, too. I'll take mine about nine-thirty, Alice," said Mr. Stewart.

They had discussed a number of things at dinner. Charles was in his Sophomore year at Stanford, Karen was in her Senior year in high school; each was absorbed with his plans for another happy school year.

Mr. Stewart was an electrical engineer, spent some of his time away from home and was always thankful to get back. His wife did some community work for the Red Cross, some church work, and kept house for their family.

"I'm pretty busy, too, if anyone should

happen to ask," said Mrs. Stewart. "If not sewing for Karen, I am doing it for the Red Cross or some missionary box. Then I do our own laundry. Thank goodness for the washers and dryers of today! I still have a little time to belong to a Study Club, and to read. Miles here brings me plenty of books." She put a hand on her oldest son's arm, and they smiled at each other.

After they had carried the food and dishes to the house, Miles and Tracy were banned from the kitchen. Miles took her on a tour of the rest of the downstairs. The living room was long, and comfortably furnished. There was a brown and beige tweed carpet, a small spinet piano, television, shelves of books and plenty of comfortable chairs; and on the left, a deep sofa of forest green. Over the fireplace hung an oil painting of a forest scene in autumnal tones of russet, gold and brown. It was a room you could live in for a long time, Tracy thought.

There was a den without curtains—they being in the process of completion—a radio, sofa and lamp table. "Sometimes we study in here, if we don't want to go to our rooms," said Miles. A desk, filled with books, writing pad and pens, a set of encyclopaedias, a student lamp, contributed to the used look of the room.

There were two bedrooms, a utility room and a "mud room," a bath and a half. "A good comfortable house," said Tracy. "One where children could grow up without bumping into each other too much."

"Space! That's what the post-war years of architecture neglected. But it's making quite a comeback."

"Verily!" said Tracy. "And now how about that walk with Belshazzer? I think I hear him whining."

"He never forgets!"

They went back out to the patio and called to the dog to follow. Seeking a well worn path, they entered the woods at the top of the hill. The moon was coming up now, a huge red ball, but Miles took a flashlight, "Just to keep away the bears!" he laughed.

He flicked it on and off until they were well on the path and the moon gave sufficient light. The woods were not as deep as Tracy had thought, some of the trees having been taken out for firewood through the years.

They walked in silence for a few minutes, Tracy breathing in deeply the scent of evergreens: cedar and pine, spruce and cypress. The path was covered with crunching needles which made their steps light and sure.

"What a wonderful place to play!" Tracy said. "I'll bet all of you enjoyed it when you were little."

"I did then, and I enjoy it now that I'm big, too!" Belshazzer gave a quick bark at that moment and leaped away in front of them, swerving off to the right.

"Well! That'll be a squirrel, I expect!" said Tracy.

"There's something about tall trees—call it perspective or what you will. I always feel a lot better after a walk in the woods. It's a good place to iron out problems and to think up ideas; so still you can hear yourself think."

They walked on silently for several yards.

"I thought I'd see more of you this week," Miles said. "And on the contrary,

175

I've seen less of you than at any time since we started dating."

"I've been awfully busy."

"Yes, I know, but I wondered if some of it was busy work, just to keep from going out with me. Did your friend object while you were at home?"

Startled, Tracy paused, and they stood facing each other on the path. "Why, yes, he did ask about you. I'd written him that we were going out together."

"And he doesn't like it? I don't blame him."

"Well, you see, we are sort of engaged. I have his pin."

"Yes, you told me that, Tracy." Very softly he added, "I hoped that it didn't mean a permanent decision."

"He's been taking out a girl lately since he's bought a new car. She's a teacher. He says that it doesn't mean anything, that she's just someone to go around with."

"I hope that isn't the way you feel about me, Tracy?"

"No, not exactly, Miles."

"And how exactly do you feel about me? I've come to miss you every moment when you're out of my sight. I was miserable last weekend, and I've been miserable all this week, thinking you were avoiding seeing me. Oh, Tracy, can't you see I've fallen in love with you?"

She couldn't say a word. A sudden trembling shook her.

He bent his head toward hers. She knew that he was going to kiss her, and she couldn't stop him. She didn't want to stop him. Then she felt his lips upon hers, and she returned the pressure and felt his arms holding her close.

"Oh, Tracy, Tracy!" he murmured.

"Miles!" They broke apart. "I shouldn't have let you kiss me!"

"But you did let me." He smiled down at her. Putting his arm around her shoulders, he turned her about, and they started back toward the house.

They had walked a long way before he spoke again. "I think you'd better warn Bob Follett that I'm going to give him a bad time. I won't give you up to him without having made some special effort to keep you."

He stooped quickly and kissed her briefly on the lips again. The second kiss caught her unawares. She closed her eyes.

She had never felt this way when Bob kissed her.

They broke through the final clearing and saw the lights of the house. Belshazzer came loping up behind them and barked eagerly at their heels.

"Okay, Bub!" grinned Miles, reaching down and patting him, "So we forgot all about you!"

15

KAREN was sleeping soundly in her twin bed when Tracy quietly let herself into the room about eleven o'clock. A panel of moonlight streamed in through the open window, and Tracy got ready for bed without turning on the lights, changing into her white pajamas she had earlier laid out on her bed.

She lay awake for almost an hour, thinking of the new developments with Miles. She hadn't meant for him to fall in love with her. It complicated things, for now she knew that it would no longer be fair to him to go out with him after this weekend, unless she acknowledged to herself that she was giving him some encouragement.

She slept soundly, waking only once when Belshazzer barked during the night. Probably at a squirrel, she thought drowsily, going back to sleep almost immediately. Karen shook her shoulder gently the next morning at seven-thirty.

179

"Miles asked me to waken you, Tracy. He said that by the time you'd breakfasted your friends will be here ready to start on your trip."

Tracy sat up slowly. "I almost forgot where I am. Yes, I promised I'd get up at seven. I hope your mother didn't get up early just to get breakfast for us," she added, scrambling into her robe.

"Don't worry. Mom and Dad are always up early, every day in the week. I expect they're waiting breakfast this morning, though, because they liked you so much."

Joining them a little later at the table in the small breakfast room, she found all the family present. They ate scrambled eggs, waffles and strawberry jam, which, to Tracy's surprise, tasted very good even at that early hour.

Iris and her friend arrived about nine, and the two couples motored almost a hundred miles down the coast and stopped to go through two of the old missions. Later they enjoyed a swim and then a picnic lunch on the beach. They had built a small fire to roast wieners and make coffee, but depended largely on ready prepared foods for the meal.

After Miles' kisses of the night before, Tracy was surprised that he did not take advantage of the situation to kiss her again, when they had all stretched out on the warm sand for a rest after their swim.

It was late when they drove back to the Stewarts' place, and Tracy stayed only a few minutes to say her appreciation for the pleasant visit and to get her overnight case.

"We hope you'll come back soon, Tracy," Miles' mother said as they shook hands. "We certainly enjoyed having you."

"I am so glad that Miles brought me, Mrs. Stewart. It's so wonderful to get a taste of family life, for I do miss it so much now."

Mr. Stewart added his friendly invitation to come again, and she felt the warmth of the whole family as she drove away with Miles.

She had told Karen to come in some Saturday with Miles; they'd spend the afternoon shopping in Union Square, and lunch at Blum's, one of their favorite places to eat. Karen had been very happy to accept the invitation, and Tracy said she hoped Karen would come soon.

The first two days of the following week, Tracy spent some time in the juvenile room, going over some of the newest books and reading reviews from the *Saturday Review, The Horn Book*, and other publications which did an excellent job of reporting on children's books. She also had some advance notices of books expected in time for Christmas sales; a big project, she realized in anyone's book shop.

Some material also came from the Children's Book Council, about which she had learned more in the Library Science Course, taken out at the University of San Francisco during the month of July. She felt that it was a worthwhile organization, and one worthy of attention when choosing books.

To her delight, she was invited to attend and serve as a consultant on juvenile literature at the University of Oregon during a Reading Workshop in late August. They would pay all expenses and thirty dollars per day for the two days that she would work on the staff.

"Gee! I'll need to bone up a bit on some

of the questions which will be asked me," she said to Aunt Ellen.

"I think it's just wonderful," said her aunt. "I'm very proud of you."

"If only I can get away from the shop!"

"But of course you can! I'll speak to Mr. Kennedy tomorrow about it."

"That's so close to the opening of school. Kids will be buying all kinds of textbooks, lots of notebooks and other school supplies!"

"Then we'll hire two or three extra people that week. We always bring in one or two, anyway!"

To her dismay, Tracy found that the two days she would need to be in Eugene would be the two days after the All Star football game in which Bob would be participating. He wouldn't be seeing much of her his first week in San Francisco, because of the practice games and training. So naturally he would want to see her immediately following the big game.

At the shop, Mr. Kennedy seemed to take delight in her invitation to serve as a consultant. "That calls for a little publicity, I'm sure. I'll get one of the boys from the *Chronicle* right on it, Miss Allen.

All of these little things do seem to be helping. It doesn't hurt, you know, for the public to realize that we have an authority on children's books right on our own staff."

Pleased that he'd spoken so kindly to her and had taken a real interest in her trip to the University, Tracy glowed with excitement. She renewed her studying of methods of displaying books and sent for several large charts and posters. She was especially interested in dramatizing the possibilities of Book Week, held annually in November, as a means of encouraging people to read. Slogans, posters, booklets and other kinds of publicity material really did help.

"But more than anything else, just making books available is the important thing," she said to Miles one morning later in the week. "I'm convinced that seeing the right book at the right moment has created an intense desire in many reluctant readers."

"You're dead right. Mom always used to bring loads of books home from the library every week when she went in to shop for the staple groceries. Food for the mind as well as for the stomach!"

"My mother did, too. She used to leave them around in every room in the house. We saw them while eating, resting, dusting and the first thing on awakening, as well as before going to sleep."

"There's nothing more disheartening to a teacher than to know many of her students' homes have no books, magazines or even newspapers in them! Of course that's practically uncivilized today—or would be, if television hadn't swept them in the background."

"Some surveys show that television has helped arouse interest in some of the older books, including the classics."

"Sometimes," grinned Miles, "I think you're practicising some of your talks on me!"

"Could be!" She smiled. "Does sound a little like a lecture, doesn't it?"

"If I don't get these books unpacked and up on the shelves, I'll be all night!" His long brown hands made short work of the job, opening the box, sorting out the titles and marking the prices.

Tracy, engrossed in sales throughout the

morning, kept her mind mostly on her work, only now and then thinking of the busy days ahead of her. Miles had asked her for a date for Thursday evening, but she had pleaded that she was too busy.

The notes in her brown leather-backed book were growing with each hour. She typed them up at spare moments, and they began to look impressively well organized. She had spent some time on research in reading problems and had gone over several articles in the *English Journal*, which the preceding winter had carried experts' suggestions in a series about secondary reading.

I have almost begun to feel like a teacher instead of a book salesman, she thought. They are something alike, of course! To know books and to know what books are for what children is a big order!

She had found several books to help her: *The Right Book For The Right Child*, bibliographies which informed her about other books.

Bob was getting impatient to get away from the Valley now, and every letter was filled with endearments and promises of

186

wonderful evenings to be spent when he arrived in San Francisco.

She did go out dancing with Miles on Saturday evening. They dined at the Sir Francis Drake, then went to the Top o' the Mark, thence to their favorite club.

"Do you know I've had a strong feeling that you've been avoiding me?" said Miles, pressing his cheek close to hers.

She looked at him laughingly. "What ever made you think that? I've been busy all week."

"Excuses, excuses!" he mumbled. "Was it because I kissed you last week, Tracy?"

Her fingers trembled within his.

"Was it?" he insisted.

"It might have been, Miles. I don't know what to do or say. If I go out with you it encourages you, and if I don't—" She broke off.

"If you don't, what?"

"Don't make me say it," she whispered.

"Say it!" he demanded.

"Well, then," she looked up at him, "I miss you like anything!"

He held her closer and whispered into her ear, "That's what I wanted to hear. What are you worrying about?"

"Bob's coming to San Francisco in one week. And he won't want me to go out with you any more."

"But how do you feel?"

"I'm not sure."

"Then why don't we just go along and do whatever we think best when the time comes? I want to see you, and I don't mean in the Book Nook, Tracy. How about going sailing with me tomorrow?"

"Okay."

"Good girl! I'll pick you up about eleven, if there's no fog. I docked down at the Marina last evening. We've a good place now, and I've a fellow looking after the boat."

"Sounds wonderful. Shall I bring lunch?"

"Some of it, if you wish."

"Fried chicken and potato salad? I think Lucy has a whole flock of little pies made up and frozen, and one will be just right for us by the time we're ready to eat it."

"Sounds swell! I'll bring the rest."

They danced until one, and then they took a drive up on their own private mountain and looked out over the sleeping city. Tracy wished that he hadn't parked, for she didn't want him to kiss her again until she had seen Bob.

He turned off the ignition, and they sat and looked at the moonlight, the few twinkling lights in apartments, the big area of light high in the sky in the downtown section.

"You know, Tracy, you fit into our family awfully well," said Miles, lighting a cigarette. "Mom and Dad were pretty crazy about you, and my kid sister has a terrific crush just from having seen you once. Even Chuck went so far as to say that, as girls go, you made a hit with him! Seems that his latest girl friend and he had a quarrel last week, so right now he's not very friendly toward the opposite sex. Belshazzer liked you, too," he added, taking her hand.

"Thanks for reporting about Belshazzer! Oh, Miles, I am so glad your family liked me. It was mutual then, for I think they're pretty wonderful. It almost seemed like home."

"We're not much society as such, but we're pretty strong for family and home ties."

"I think that's the best possible kind of life."

"Tracy, will you marry me?" He leaned over and tipped her chin up so that the moonlight fell upon her soft cheeks.

"Oh, Miles!" she said softly.

They just looked at each other for a long moment. Then she added, "I'm engaged to Bob. It's too soon for you to ask me . . . I don't know what to say."

"Are you sure about Bob?"

He could hardly hear her answer. "I'm not really. I don't know why I took his pin."

Miles drew away from her. "I know it's not ethical to ask a girl to marry you when she's already engaged, but somehow I get the impression that you are not really in love with Bob."

Doubts rose within her, washing over her, drowning her with indecision. Bob was not like the ideal she had pictured in her girlhood.

"Maybe we'd better go now," she said softly.

"All right," he agreed. They were silent as he drove into the city, and silent all the way to her Aunt Ellen's house.

"And how about tomorrow's sail?" he asked as he walked with her to the front door.

"How do you feel about it?"

"I'd like to go if you would. Nothing like a fine day of sailing to clear the cobwebs out of one's brains."

She laughed. "I don't know whether to feel insulted or not."

"Oh, I meant my own. I don't know what makes me so stupid, pressing every chance for an advantage. Well, you can count on me to bide my time, Tracy. I won't try to kiss you again unless I think you want me to!"

She laughed lightly. "It's a deal. I've only known you about two months, Miles."

"Yes. Yes, I had that coming. Well, I'm a patient man."

His words followed her as she turned out the night lamp and went on upstairs. Was he really a patient man? And how patient was Bob? She got out his last letter and re-read it. He didn't sound very patient to her.

191

16

THE following Monday morning, Tracy arrived at the Book Nook earlier than usual. By now she had her own front door key, one that her Aunt Ellen had insisted she have duplicated when she had been caught in a downpour one morning when Mr. Kennedy was late. She entered by herself today and, going over to the fireplace, turned on the heat, to ward off some of the weekend chill.

The big shop was quiet. It would be half an hour until Mr. Kennedy would get there. Suddenly she realized that by hurrying she could probably get down to the vaults, make a quick investigation and return before the manager arrived.

In a moment she had entered the main office and, finding all the keys on the board, took the ones marked "Vault Doors." Going down the basement steps quietly, she turned on the overhead light. The steps were narrow and the passage dark. She remembered them very well for they contributed to the feeling of mystery she had always associated with the vaults in the old days.

The large outer door opened heavily, needing oiling. Inside, she found steel doors and, turning the key into the lock, found they opened easily and noiselessly.

A cold, dank smell greeted her. She didn't recall that it used to be damp down there.

She frowned a little, knowing that dampness could soon ruin precious volumes. She found the light switch and turned it on. A brisk sale of books must have been going on for some time, because there were not as many filled shelves as she recalled.

Her first move was to take down a nearby book and to sniff at it. A feeling of dismay touched her. These books were badly in need of airing and warmth and dry shelves. She touched the heater and found it cold. Involuntarily, she turned the heat on to its lowest temperature, and then began a quick survey of the nearest books.

One of them was the *Secret Diary of the Southern General* which she recalled seeing upstairs in the anteroom at one time. There were others just as fascinating. A new stack that had not been shelved stood on the small table in the center of the very small room. The safe was locked, she found, and, not knowing the combination of the lock, she turned back to the shelves. Glancing at her watch, she saw she'd been gone ten minutes. Not daring to risk spending further time there, she turned out the lights and retraced her steps, locking both doors behind her.

Her heart beating hard, she regained the main salesroom and then rehung the keys in the office where she'd found them.

Having done all this, she really didn't know that she'd accomplished anything. What good did it do to snoop around if she didn't know exactly what to look for? Nothing would be of any real value except to see the records and to judge whether or not the profits were enough to balance the sales.

Only the accountant and Aunt Ellen's attorney can really be of much value at this particular time, and only if she has their complete confidence and their loyalty. Of course that would be true of her aunt's attorney, but what about the accountant?

Wasn't it possible that if anything dishonest was being carried on he could be a partner to it, and actually be covering up the records of the sales?

She knew that her aunt had talked recently with her attorney, when the first of the month had not shown any material increase in the profits. She had not told Tracy of the outcome of their conference, excepting to say that the attorney would have another talk with her soon. In the meantime Tracy was to watch as much as possible, check on items that she knew were coming into the shop in the way of unusual purchases, and if possible note the names of people who were having private conferences with Mr. Kennedy.

She was writing orders at the main desk when Mr. Kennedy came in. Miles followed him shortly, his arms loaded with packages from the post office. These were the smaller daily unexpected packages; boxes were brought in by the delivery truck almost daily, too.

Still feeling a bit shaky after having secretly visited the vaults, Tracy worked hard at the task before her. She kept her eyes on her typing and on the small catalogue from which she was taking titles.

Miles opened packages, distributed the personal mail for them and took care of customers as usual. He brought one or two unusual advertising folders over to her desk between customers, and commented upon them.

"Gosh, but you're the busy little bee!" he said in dismay.

"Just earning my salary," she said airily. "See you at coffee time?"

"Right. Need to talk about our sail of yesterday."

A warm feeling stole over her. She had had a wonderful time with him, and she had a pink nose to attest to her sojourn on the Bay.

The days would pass very quickly and summer would soon be over, although she sometimes thought there was very little sharp changes in seasons on the Coast, until the fog blew in cold and dreary.

At about ten o'clock the girl Myrna came in. Avoiding the main desk, she started toward Mr. Kennedy's private office.

Tracy rose swiftly and, going forward,

said, "May I help you?" She smiled sweetly.

"I'd like to see Mr. Kennedy, please," the girl said crisply. She tossed the end of her stole, and Tracy had to try hard to keep from smiling at the sight of her impatience at being stopped.

"Do you have an appointment?" Tracy asked sweetly.

Myrna's dark eyes flashed. "I hardly think I need one, miss."

And that puts me in my place, I suppose.

"Just have a chair and I'll ask him if he can see you now."

The girl frowned, but kept moving toward the door. Tracy maneuvered a bit and stood in front of her. "I'm sorry, but I think you'll need to wait a moment. Who shall I say is calling?"

"Miss Allen!" sharply from Mr. Kennedy's door. Then in a softer tone, "Yes, Miss Allen, I'm expecting her. Come in."

And that's that! Tracy thought, going back to her desk. At any rate, I did what Aunt Ellen suggested. I tried to get her name. She was not carrying anything. Nor had she been the other time she had come to see Mr. Kennedy.

A thought clicked in Tracy's mind. They could of course deliver books in the evenings. But why risk using the Book Nook at all?

Solely for the prestige and for the access to the clients' names, of course. But by this time, Mr. Kennedy could have made lists of them, could have carried on enough business so that he really had no need of the store.

Just then Miles interrupted her soliloquy to ask her to go to coffee with him. But Kennedy had just gone down to the vaults. When he returned, she wanted to be there to see if he had a book.

She pleaded that she had to finish her task first. "Later?" she asked Miles beguilingly. "Anyway, we can't leave the store alone. Mr. Kennedy's busy with the girl Myrna right now."

"Who's she?"

Tracy shook her head, indicating that she didn't know and that it probably wasn't important. "Why don't you run along? I don't think we can make it together, anyway. And I do want to get this out of the way while I'm in the mood."

"Mrs. Gaither's list?"

"Yes, for all the nieces and nephews for Christmas, and about fifty books for the orphanage she's interested in."

"Wonderful person, Mrs. Gaither." Miles buttoned up his coat. "I didn't stop for breakfast, so I'll run along."

He had been gone almost long enough to be coming back when the private office door opened and Myrna came out, bearing a wrapped package. Without a glance toward Tracy, she sailed quickly out of the store. Mr. Kennedy sat at his desk, busy with a letter.

What's in that package? Tracy asked herself. I can find out tomorrow morning if I get here early enough.

She was so absorbed in her work that she didn't go out for coffee at all that morning, and so took an early lunch hour. She and Iris Langdon met as usual and ate their usual lunch—a salad and a roll and a glass of milk.

They walked in the bright sunlight for half an hour in the Square, and Tracy felt relief from the pressure of the morning's excitement. She decided that she wouldn't discuss the girl Myrna with her Aunt Ellen. There was no need to worry her with anything this specific unless she was certain that there was something which needed investigation.

None of the incidents added up to anything positive yet.

"You know, you seem very thoughtful today," said Iris as they were parting. "Everything going all right at the shop?"

"As usual," said Tracy, which really did not commit her.

"See you tomorrow then. Maybe I'll go to I. Magnin's and look at suits. Want to come along, if we can get served an early lunch?"

"Of course. We could call in our order and have it ready."

"Yes, we can do that," said Iris. "I'll see you."

When she returned to the shop Miles went out for lunch, and she was left alone in the building with Kennedy. She sensed that he had come out of his office and was studying her in a serious fashion.

He walked slowly over to the desk. She was certain that he was going to speak to her and she wondered if she had offended him.

Just on the verge of speaking to her, he paused as someone came in from the street. Rising, she went to ask to help the customer, and Kennedy said quietly, "Oh, I'll go to lunch, Miss Allen."

She nodded. Helping the customer, who wanted to buy a copy of C. Y. Lee's *Flower Drum Song*, she wrapped it and accepted the money automatically.

As the customer left the store, a sudden horrifying thought came to Tracy.

I left the heat on in the vault. At this moment she couldn't understand why she had even turned it on. But maybe it wouldn't have been noticed. The chances were that Mr. Kennedy had turned it off last week and forgotten to put it back on again.

Would he have noticed it? She tried to tell herself that he probably hadn't. But she was very nervous during the afternoon, and sensed Kennedy's eyes upon her several times studying her thoughtfully.

I can't let such things bother me, or I'll be a nervous wreck, she thought as she went home on the bus.

She was glad to get off at her bus stop and walk the two short blocks. It was good to get out into the open air, because her head was throbbing a little. There was a snap in the cool air tonight. It began to feel as though fall were around the corner.

17

AUGUST passed swiftly, the days rushing past. Bob arrived in San Francisco and found that his training took most of his attention. During the week of the All Star game, Tracy went to Eugene as planned and served on the Reading Workshop as juvenile literature consultant.

While there she received a corsage from Miles Stewart to wear to the dinner where a national authority, Paul Witty, spoke on the Improvement of Reading. It was very like Miles to send her the corsage and very like Bob not to realize the dinner was an important one.

The two days away from the shop were soul-satisfying to Tracy. She had not realized how tense she had become, listening for undercurrents which might indicate trouble brewing, nor had she realized that she was constantly avoiding Miles even at work.

She had spent one night at home with

her family and flew back to San Francisco the next day, having four days away from the city. She enjoyed the work at the University. To her surprise, she was asked to serve on another workshop the following spring in Portland. Although she was not certain yet, she tentatively accepted the invitation.

Bob was out of town the first two weeks in September, and Tracy refused Miles' invitation to spend another weekend at his home. A large community barbecue was to be held, and his parents were two of the official hosts, and had thought Tracy would enjoy coming to the affair.

"I would enjoy it, Miles. Please tell them I do appreciate their asking me, but I've promised Aunt Ellen I'll help entertain guests this weekend."

It was true, but she felt guilty using it as an excuse, for she could easily have been given permission to go.

She had gone out with Miles only three times since their day sailing on the Bay. Bob had made it perfectly clear that now that he was in the city, he didn't want her dating anyone else.

September had brought the shop the

rush which they had expected, and the staff was temporarily enlarged to five. Two substitutes were needed anyway, to carry on during staff vacations next year, and to help out in the holiday rush. The volume of business would certainly more than take care of the additional salaries.

One of the girls who had been hired was little more than a high school graduate with only meager sales experience, and after trying to teach her how to handle customers, Tracy gave over several of the routine jobs to her and took over the sales work as much as possible. Miles and the new young man were kept very busy, too, and even Mr. Kennedy helped out during the busiest part of the day.

"I'm sorry you've been working so hard, dear," Aunt Ellen said the last of September. "The volume of business this year has been tremendous. It did help for you to do your work in the juvenile field this summer. Mr. Kennedy says that much of the fiction business for children seems to be a direct result of your interest and work."

"I'm glad of that. It was kind of Mr. Kennedy to tell you. It has been a hard month, but things are bound to level off a bit now that we're going into the second month of school."

"When will your young man be out to the house again? I mean Bob, of course. I thought you'd like to ask him for dinner. Mattie does enjoy cooking for a man."

"Yes, I'll ask him the next time we have a date. He's going to Cleveland next week. In the meantime I don't get to see much of him because of the game here Saturday."

"You'll attend, won't you?"

"Not this time, Auntie. I will the next home game."

She had gone to one of them, but she had sat alone, not even asking Miles to go, although she felt that it would have been fun. He had gone with his brother, she learned afterward; she never knew that he had sat immediately above her five rows back.

"Charles and I ate hot dogs and drank pop just like we used to do. We had a swell time. Bob's quite a man!" he had said the following Monday at work. He meant it, too, which was rather big of him, Tracy thought.

The fall brought weather problems too,

and Tracy found herself occasionally accepting a ride from Bob in the evenings, so that if it rained she didn't have to walk the distance from the bus stop to her aunt's house.

"It's hardly out of my way," Bob said, "and it's ridiculous for you to get off the bus in the driving rain and to get your feet wet. Having to wait on the bus and then stand up, too, is no joke."

Tracy accepted the rides more and more gratefully in late November, for the weather grew more unpredictable.

Bob was seeing her more frequently now, and they saw a number of the shows together and ate out occasionally. He shared a large apartment with three other men, and they invited three girls and Tracy for a dinner party one Saturday evening.

Tracy went early and arranged flowers, having picked up some beautiful bronze mums and greens near Union Square. The dinner was to be served buffet style on a long counter in the end of the large living room. There was a hearth and a pair of tan leather benches where they could sit to eat. It was a rather handsome place, Tracy thought, noting the thick pile of the carpet, the polished brass fire set and the deep chairs and luxurious ottomans. There were four bedrooms, two baths and the kitchen.

"Like it?" Bob asked, holding her hand as they went through the place.

"Yes, very much. It's quite masculine-looking."

"Guess it's been used for several years by bachelors on the team. We pay a good price for the use of it, so it should be fairly nice. Maid service, garages, and everything else very convenient."

She met the other three men as they came straggling in: Hank Stevens, Mel D'arcy, Tim Kittridge. All husky, athletic types and congenial, she presumed, since they'd been staying together now for three months or more.

"Kinda gets me, this weather," said Tim. "Oughta be out there limbering up, but the field's just like a swamp."

"We'll use the gym tomorrow if this downpour keeps up."

"How long've you known this guy?" asked Mel, indicating Bob to Tracy.

"Long enough to know better," she said, adjusting a flower.

"Like I told you, he certainly must have had you fooled!" said Hank. "When are our girls getting here?"

"About six-thirty," said Tim. "They're all coming out together in one taxi. Real chummy."

Two of the girls were sisters, Alison and Kitty Myers, and the other girl was a neighbor whom they had included as a blind date with Hank.

"Better start getting this show on the road if we're to eat at seven or even eight," said Mel. Taking off his jacket, he went into the kitchen prepared to wrestle with ingredients for the bouillabaisse which he had volunteered to make.

When she went out to join those in the kitchen later, Tracy saw why it took so long to prepare. Interesting trays of various seafoods stood around waiting to be added to the aromatic pot bubbling on the range.

Mel, wearing a large white apron, stood stirring, and reading the recipe at the same time.

"It says here, 'One whole crab, cracked,

one-half lobster, two pounds of little neck clams, two dozen prawns, cooked and peeled . . ." He broke off and, going to the counter, counted the prawns. "They're spiced, and if one of you sons of guns eat another, there won't be enough. Now lay off 'em, won't you?"

"I told you to get double the amount. I'll run over to Barnacle Bill's and get some more if we need 'em, Stingy."

"What else goes into that brew?" asked Tracy, entranced. "I've eaten it at the Old Portland when I was a child, but Mother never did make it at home."

"—One pound of red snapper or white fish, one pound of halibut, a dozen shrimp and one dozen scallops," Mel continued reading as though he'd not interrupted himself. "Of course there are other things like leeks and parsley, paprika, thyme, and don't forget the saffron."

"Nor the sauterne," observed Tim, tipping the bottle as though to drink it.

"All in good time," said Mel. "First the vegetables have to be browned in the olive oil, and—"

"Come on, Tracy; don't listen any more. I've got to finish these crackers and open-faced sandwiches for the *hors d'oeuvres*. Come help me," said Bob.

The girls arrived at seven, only half an hour late, and just when the men had decided they weren't coming after all.

"It took us longer than we expected," said Kitty, her blue eyes laughing at Tim. "We got lost like I said we would. I wanted to get a taxi, as you suggested, but no, we had to drive!"

"'S all right now. Come on and take your coats off and get up here by the fire."

It had been so long since Tracy had been out with several couples in one party that she felt grateful to Bob.

As the evening wore on, they ate heartily of the food, the men drank all of the cocktails and had to make more, and the girls cleared up the table for them. The two sisters and their dates left soon after eleven, for they had planned on going to a night club to dance. By this time Hank had had too much to drink, and so Bob put him to bed.

Soon after eleven they took the other girl home, and then Bob went in Tracy's house for a little chat before returning to his apartment.

"I'm afraid it wasn't too good a party, Honey," he said.

"Why, I thought it was quite nice, Bob." She could even excuse Hank. He didn't ordinarily date girls, Bob had said, since he had been married once and had been divorced.

"A member of a pro team doesn't always make a good marriage bet," Bob said tonight as he and Tracy sat on the sofa in the den where a low fire still burned in the grate.

"Does Hank think his profession interfered with his?"

"In a way, yes. However, he also said that it hadn't been a good marriage even when he signed up. I suppose they found they weren't suited, and the kind of life he led just wasn't conducive to a good marriage. Unfortunately, they had a couple of children."

"Poor Hank! And poor children!"

"Yeah, it's sort of bad sometimes. He gets letters now and then from the little girl. She's in the second grade, and we can always tell when he gets one. She prints her letters so funny; you know how kids' letters look."

She nodded. "Where do they live?"

"In Idaho some place. He may go home for Christmas."

"Where will you be during the holidays, Bob?"

"Here, I hope, although we may get a game at Miami."

"Maybe I could fly down for it if you go."

"That would be wonderful. We'll sure count on it."

It was something nice to dream about. She'd never made any journey farther away from home than an occasional Coast trip; once the family had gone to Yellowstone Park when she was about sixteen. How long ago that seemed now!

Bob left about twelve-thirty. He made no date for the next week, for his leisure schedule was uncertain. "Honey, I'm sorry. I thought we'd have lots more time together than we have had," he said as he kissed her good night.

"It's all right, Bob. Gives me a sort of clue, too, to the kind of life we'd be living."

"Don't get any funny ideas that you

might not like it, Babe!" He chucked her under the chin playfully.

She smiled at him and didn't attempt any comment. But she remembered what Hank had said—that following a ball team didn't make for a very good kind of a marriage. It must be hard on the wives and the children. What could one do after the babies came? Settle down in a town close to the training quarters and learn to live with loneliness?

18

THE holiday rush seemed to start earlier than usual this year; orders began to roll in soon after Thanksgiving.

"The whole country is getting education-minded!" exclaimed Miles one blustery morning early in December.

"Well, with all the blasts last year in most of the major magazines about how superior Russian education is, and all the talk about adjusting curricula and why Johnny can't read, et cetera, there was bound to be a reformation in the reading world. Everyone must have books, and I'm all for it!" laughed Tracy. "You should see my scrap book. It's filled with articles from *This Week*, *The Post*, and all the women's magazines."

"But most of the earlier blasts have been softened now that we have almost caught up with the ICB program. Still, as you say, we have become book-conscious. Say, did

215

you see the new decorations in Magnin's windows?"

"No, Aunt Ellen brought me, and I came in the back way this morning."

"Go to lunch early, then, and take a look. They're mighty handsome. Makes me feel all Christmasy. Which is one way to bring up the fact that you're invited to a tree-decorating party at our house Christmas Eve."

"Oh, Miles! How nice!"

"You'll come, then?" He glowed.

She was thinking rapidly. Bob had said if they had a game at Miami that she must fly down for it. But what would it be like to sit among strangers watching a football game in bright sunlight? But of course, Silly, it won't be until after Christmas Day.

Bob will be gone Christmas Eve, too. He'll have to leave early. But what of your folks? They'll expect you at home. She said to Miles, "I was just thinking of complications. My folks, of course, expect me home, and then, too, I might possibly fly to Miami."

"Oh." Miles looked crestfallen. "Well,

for a moment I forgot about your folks and that you'd probably be going home."

"I've never been away from home for Christmas," she said slowly. "Of course there's always a first time, and then, too, I'll probably be needed at the shop. I can remember how it used to look at home on Christmas Eve. All the bookstores' shelves would be practically empty; all the gift boxes and all the merchandise gone! I probably shouldn't count on going home until Christmas Day. I could catch a plane that morning."

"Of course you could. And after we soak our feet in hot water for two hours after closing time," they laughed, "then there'd still be time to come to my house."

"I'll certainly think about it, and I do think it's lovely to be included."

They busied themselves putting new books on shelves for most of the next hour. Stopping beside her finally to survey their work, Miles said, "I've been intending to talk with you, Tracy, about something you brought up once." He cast a quick look toward the main office where Kennedy was working at the desk.

"Oh?" Startled, Tracy followed his gaze.

"Think we could go out to coffee together?"

"Why not? The other two can look after the customers. It's slackening off a bit now." She glanced at her watch. "I've not been going out, but I think we could certainly spare ten or fifteen minutes today."

Somehow, as she slipped into her coat, she knew that he was thinking of Kennedy and the rare books.

Things had never been any better as far as profits were concerned. Of course there had been a spurt of business in the early fall, and one was expected now during holiday sales, but as far as the valuable book sales were concerned, there had not been enough of an increase to be felt.

They walked quietly to the small coffee shop where they found their usual table by a window.

After ordering sweet rolls and coffee for them, Miles lit a cigarette. "I've wanted to ask you if your aunt's attorney was able to help her. We've never discussed it since you mentioned it to me once."

"We've not discussed it at home, either, lately. I sometimes think that Aunt Ellen has decided that her husband was unusually capable in that direction, and is resigned to a smaller profit from the shop. I must confess that I've not noticed anything particularly doubtful, although I still don't understand why I am never asked anything about rare books."

"That's what I wanted to mention, too. It does seem to me that by this time, one or two clients would surely have approached you or me or both of us. But the only time someone did, as far as I'm concerned it was an accident. It was a telephone call. I heard the soft, gentle voice of an elderly woman, and when I said, 'The Book Nook,' she began to talk about a very old book she had discovered among her father's effects. She said, 'Mr. Kennedy, I'm sure that it is one that you'd like to buy.'"

"Mr. Kennedy?"

Miles nodded. "I said before thinking, 'Mr. Kennedy is out just now, but I'll give him your message.' And you know, Tracy, her voice showed great agitation. 'No, No!

Please young man, don't. I'll call again. Thank you.' Then she hung up."

"And what did you do?"

"It happened just last week, Tracy. I'm still mulling it over in my mind. Ethically, I wonder if I shouldn't just keep quiet about it."

"Do you think she did call again?"

"How could we possibly tell? He gets many calls each day."

"That's right. Also, did you know that I no longer have an extension line? My phone has been changed over to an outside line."

"Mine, too. It must have been done at night recently. Nothing was mentioned about it."

"Do you think that he knows she called, then?"

Miles nodded. "Yes. I think that's why the lines were changed. It's really quite a handicap. Old-fashioned as all get out, to have to answer each other's phones when we could all be on one or two."

They ate the rolls and drank their coffee in silence. Tracy was thinking rapidly.

Of course we have been lulled into this because we were so busy in September, and also because of the care with which he seems to make his sales.

She had never been able to go back into the vault since that one time, although she had planned on following through with her plan to go check the shelves the day after Myrna was there.

"I've not seen anything of that girl, Myrna, for weeks," she said now to Miles.

"I've wondered if she might just be a friend calling at the shop."

"Have you ever seen Mr. Kennedy's wife?"

"Yes. She's a small blonde. She's not Myrna, if that's what you were wondering about. He certainly is very close about his family and home life. I think there's a boy or two and a small girl of eighteen months or so".

"I don't even know where they live. They moved in the fall, but Mr. Kennedy didn't mention it. There was a change of address requested, and I left him a note".

"Very uncommunicative. But then, of course, lots of businessmen want it that way. They don't care to mix social, business and personal lives."

She nodded. It must be a rather strange

way to live. Imagine her parents living a sequestered life—one in which there was no admixture of business! Why, her father often went back to the store to get a neighbor a pan or a sack of fertilizer he happened to mention over the back yard fence in the course of an evening.

"Time's up!" said Miles, looking at his watch.

"Thanks for telling me about the telephone call."

"I had to," he said simply.

But he didn't mention anything about it again during the next few weeks.

At the last moment Bob decided that it would be a mistake for Tracy to fly to Miami for the game. "If we could go together, or if we could be together much, it would be different. But you'd miss your family Christmas, and it means a lot to you."

"It's very thoughtful of you to consider that. Of course, I am disappointed."

"Go if you want to, then. But the manager said last night that we'd be flying back the next day. He's chartered a plane. There won't be any banquet the night of the game, for most of the fellows will be too worn out. You know how it is after a big one!"

By now she knew. He sometimes dropped to sleep by ten o'clock, and she realized that exhaustion was more demanding than romance. One of the vocational hazards, he had said ruefully the first time she'd gently awakened him to send him home after he'd slept forty minutes.

She wrote her parents that she planned to spend Christmas Eve in San Francisco, since she'd be working all that day, and then to fly home the next morning. There was a long distance call and some packages to slip under her aunt's tree. Her folks were very understanding. It would be nice to get home again.

The last day in the shop was perfectly murderous, she afterward reported to her aunt. Pale and wan, she came in from the bus at five.

"Miles sent me home early. He insisted they could finish, and I didn't argue."

"You look really ill." Aunt Ellen fluttered around. "Come and take a good hot bath and I'll bring you some hot broth, dear."

"I'll be all right as soon as I soak my feet! I know what we mean now when we talk about vocational hazards!"

Wrapped in a bright red woolen robe after her hot bath, she stretched out in a big chair by the fireplace in the den. She sipped hot beef broth, wriggled her toes in warm water as prescribed and sank back, enjoying the luxury of feeling babied.

She and her aunt ate an early dinner so that she could dress and be ready by seven-thirty when Miles came for her.

She wore a new bright red party dress, feeling by now in the holiday spirit. Her conscience had nagged at her while she dressed. You're more excited than you should be about going over to Mill Valley with the Stewart family tonight. You really should not have accepted Miles' invitation, for Bob thinks you are safely at home.

Dressing her hair high on her forehead and adding a touch of perfume behind her ears, putting her arms into the sleeves of her new fur jacket which Ellen had given her in time to wear tonight, she continued to feel buoyant.

When the chimes rang, she went to the door herself, letting Miles into the bright hall. He had somehow managed to renew himself without going home from the shop and then driving all the distance back.

"You look like the Spirit of Christmas! And not any Dickens character, either," he said, stopping her under the light and pivoting her around. "In fact, you look very wonderful!"

"Not as though I'd just returned from the salt mines?"

"No! Just as though you'd been napping and resting for hours. Wait a minute, now. Stand still." He fumbled in his pocket and, reaching over her head with one hand and tipping up her chin with the other, kissed her soundly.

"Miles!" she gasped.

"It's an old American custom," he explained, showing her what he had held above her head. "Mistletoe, you know. I've been carrying it around all day, but never did get a chance to tack it over the door."

19

THE warmth and affection in the Stewart household acted like a charm on Tracy, soothing her nerves, lulling her into a state of happiness such as she'd not known since leaving her home town. The evening spun like a crazy tinseled top. Decorating the tree was the main event, participated in by all the family and followed by a cup of hot oyster stew and coffee and fruit cake at midnight.

The spruce logs were burning brightly, the lights on the tree twinkled from in front of the picture window, and the white dog, Belshazzer, lay sleeping on the hearth rug. Alone in the room for a few minutes while Mrs. Stewart and Karen cleared the refreshment trays, Tracy and Miles sat looking into the fireplace.

Dreams and castles, castles and dreams, Tracy thought a bit drowsily. "Christmas was always so important at our house, too," she said. "Dad observed an old custom which had been followed in his family for generations. On the stroke of twelve, he would shout, 'Christmas Gift!' It seems that it was important to be the first to say it, so we all caught on while fairly young, and he had competition. I can just see them tonight."

"Homesick?"

She nodded. "But not as much as I'd have been if I'd flown to Miami."

"That subject is tabu!"

"I know. I'm just glad I'm here, Miles."

"That makes two of us. More, counting my folks." He reached for her hand and held it and, leaning over, kissed her. Drawing her closely to him, he kissed her again, and she responded.

Belshazzer barked softly. They moved apart as Charles came into the room with an armload of wood.

"Better not put any more on, Charles. I think this will probably last till bedtime. Tracy has a plane to catch tomorrow, and I've promised not to keep her up too late."

"Okay. I was just doing my daily Boy Scout deed. C'mon, 'Shazzer; it's time to seek your kennel. Good night, you two, and a Merry Christmas to you, Tracy, if I don't see you before you leave."

227

She rose and, going over beside him, said, "Charles, if you get up to the University any time and have a chance, please go see my folks."

"I may go up on the basketball team in February, and I sure will try to see them."

Mrs. Stewart, Karen and Mr. Stewart came into the room just then to say good night.

On the plane flying toward home the next day, Tracy kept thinking of the evening and how much like her own people the Stewarts seemed to be. They had good solid backgrounds, an appreciation for culture and a home life that was deeply satisfying.

Bob had not known of her decision to spend Christmas Eve with Miles, and she felt a little guilty that she had not told him. Yet she consoled herself by thinking that he would probably have worried a little about it and perhaps have been angry. It certainly wouldn't have helped his playing in the game.

The big game would start about two o'clock, just the time she and her family would be sitting down to the annual turkey feast.

She read a little, caught a short nap and spent the remainder of the time thinking of the situation at the shop, and of Bob and Miles.

After last evening, she felt a little numb whenever she thought of what would happen when she refused Miles his next request for a date. She didn't really want to refuse his invitation. He had said, "I'll meet your plane when you return, so be sure and let me know what time you'll arrive."

"I'm not sure yet when I'll come, Miles." Her aunt had suggested that she spend the week before New Year's with her parents, but Tracy knew she was badly needed in the shop.

"But there will be practically no sales, dear. No one has any money after Christmas."

"Inventory, though, Aunt Ellen. Mr. Kennedy says it's the best time to take it, while stocks are low and before we get busy again."

Being back in San Francisco would present a problem to her. Bob would want her to attend the New Year's Ball at the

St. Francis. Miles had invited her, too, for the same occasion.

She had put them both off by saying she wasn't sure she'd be back in time for it.

"Oh, but you have to be back, Honey," Bob had said.

"Aren't you going home at all during the holidays?"

"I haven't anything in Seattle," Bob said a little shortly. "I like to feel independent. The folks always go out for New Year's. I can remember when I was little, I used to listen to all the whistles and the bells and wish I could go, too. But I always had a baby sitter."

Bob hadn't had too happy a childhood, she realized.

As the plane approached Portland, she felt a rising excitement. Other passengers were getting ready to disembark, and so she got her packages down from the shelf, put on fresh lipstick and her new, pert red hat.

Today her father and Tom met the plane. Her mother and the girls were home preparing the dinner for which an uncle and aunt from Denver had flown in unexpectedly the day before.

230

"Did Mom know they were to be here?" Tracy asked after getting herself and her luggage settled into the family station wagon.

"They wired us just before they took off that they were flying to Portland and that we should meet them if convenient, and your Mother had a picnic getting ready for them."

Home, family, warmth, hospitality, and love. "I can hardly wait to get there," said Tracy, "and to see the folks, all of them. Did I get any presents?" She smiled at Tom.

"Not a thing! You weren't expecting any, now were you?"

The bantering, chatter about the job, school, business, the delights waiting at home, occupied the driving time. When they turned in at the driveway, the house spilled out the two girls, and her mother was not far behind them as they ran across the lawn to greet Tracy.

Tracy had her usual gifts, some that had come to her aunt's house in San Francisco. They included a new quilted housecoat, slippers and pajamas, a handsome new sweater, a manicure set, cologne, perfume.

"What did Bob get you?" demanded Leslie.

"He's bringing it from Miami."

"You mean he has time to go shopping?" asked Tom.

"Possibly."

Tracy changed the subject. Her aunt and uncle seemed happy at being with the family and praised the good job the Allens had done in bringing up the children.

"I just can't get over your being so grown up!" Her uncle beamed at Tracy. "You were just a tadpole the last time I went fishing with you in the creek near our ranch. Remember?"

"Indeed I do! And I caught a small trout. Rainbow, I think you said?"

"Right, and Aunt Helen cooked it for you, and you ate it in five minutes flat, saying it was the best thing you ever tasted."

"Must have been the Colorado mountain air," laughed her aunt.

"Excitement in those days just plain made me starved. But I remember it was good."

They watched the game later on television. Bob played well, and Tracy was proud of him.

"He plays a pretty good game," said Tom approvingly when Bob caught a long pass. "I read that the Pittsburgh Pirates are trying to buy him."

Tracy's heart missed a beat. "You did?"

"Sure. It was in yesterday's paper. They've been watching him for some time. They've offered a good round sum, too. Gosh, Sis, didn't Bob tell you? He's bound to have known."

"No. He hasn't said anything about it."

"Probably wondered why you hadn't noticed it. Don't you ever read the sports section?"

"Not lately," she said ruefully. "We've been too busy."

"Well, gosh! Tracy, that's not very flattering to Bob!" said Susan.

"On the other hand, I don't expect him to read all the book reviews!" Tracy defended herself with spirit. "I'll bet he hasn't read a *Saturday Review* since coming to San Francisco, nor before then either."

"Gosh!" Tom stared at her. "You don't expect him to, do you?"

"Certainly not. But neither should I be expected to read all of the sports section!"

"Sh! Commercial's over now; let's get on with the game," said Leslie.

So Bob might be leaving the West Coast! Baseball had always interested him. He had done very well in that popular sport at the University, too. She had known that he had one or two offers the last spring that he played.

But he ate, talked, dreamed football. She watched until the end of the half, then went to help her mother.

"Don't you want to see the rest of the game, dear?"

"No, just to hear how it comes out, I guess. Of course I love football, but I don't want to miss being with you as much as I can." She gave her mother a quick kiss. "It's so good to be home, Mom."

"Can't you give up that job and come home for the rest of the winter, Tracy? We surely do miss you. And you know you could work in the Library here."

"It wouldn't be half so interesting. I still have a job to do."

They talked about Ellen Taylor's health,

the bookshop, Bob, and a little about Miles and his family.

Tracy was not aware how her face lighted as she told of the evening she'd spent with them, and of the weekend when she had been their guest.

"Sound like a wonderful family. Charles reminds me of Tom," said her mother.

Tracy decided to spend three days at home, and called her aunt the next day to tell her.

"Dear, you've had about five calls from two different young men. Bob, of course, and also Mr. Stewart."

"But Mr. Stewart knew that I wouldn't be back today."

"Oh, he just called once. The other four tries were from Miami, long distance."

"But Bob knew I planned on coming home."

"Yes, dear." Aunt Ellen's gentle voice added, "I reminded him."

Tracy knew then that Bob had been celebrating the victory of his team and must have been drinking.

"Did you talk to him personally?"

"Yes, he cut in on the operator and insisted on talking with you. Kept asking when you'd get back. He called once on Christmas Eve."

"Oh, I see. Aunt Ellen, did you tell him I was at Miles' home?"

"No, dear. I just told him to try your Dad's home on Christmas Day."

"Well, thank you, Auntie Ellen. Then you say he called your house again?"

"Three more times, dear; last night, that was."

She knew that sooner or later he'd be calling her here, perhaps as soon as the chartered plane landed in San Francisco with the team.

She wandered a little aimlessly about the house, refusing an invitation from her sisters to go downtown shopping to take advantage of the marvelous sales.

"I have to spend my Christmas check, you know," said Susan. "And Knowles have the dreamiest sweaters advertised in their Top Buys of the week."

"I'm waiting for a call from Bob."

"Do you think he'll go to the Pirates?" asked Sue.

"I hope not," said Tracy. It would mean his leaving the Coast almost at once.

But it would mean a lot more than that,

too, she thought. It would also mean her leaving the Coast and giving up her job sometime next summer. She would be far away from her family and her life with books would be over.

All this was more or less confirmed a bit later when Bob did get a call through. However, it was not until the second day after Christmas. She had just finished eating dinner with the family and was sitting with Leslie, listening to some new records for the Hi Fi, when the telephone rang.

"It's for you, Sis! Trace!" called Tom. "It's Bob, I think."

The two girls, Leslie and Susan, came running, and Tom leaned against the hall door.

Tracy stood with her hand cupped over the mouthpiece of the telephone. "All of you just go peddle your papers, please. This is to be a private conversation."

"I'll listen in on the den phone."

"Better yet, I'll just take it in the den," said Tracy. "Now, scoot, all three of you! Mother—" she called.

"Hi, darling," said Bob. "Gosh, but you're hard to get. Where've you been?"

"Right here at 10 Linden Drive for the past few days, almost by the phone."

"Good! Nothing like having a pretty girl waiting for you!" He was the same old exuberant Bob when things were going well with him. "Well, Honey, you should start bracing yourself. I've got news to tell you. Lots of news, Baby."

"Yes, Bob?" A little sickening lurch shook her.

"Hello, Tracy, are you there? Oh, I can hear you now. I said I've got news for you. Ready?"

"Do I need any special preparation?" she stalled.

"Not if you can pack your bag in a hurry. How would you like to get married next week and go to Philadelphia for a honeymoon?"

"Why, Bob!"

"Don't wail at me, Honey. Is it yes or no?"

"But, Bob, you take my breath away. The last time we talked about it, we said not sooner than next June, remember?"

"I can't hear you, Tracy."

She repeated her words, realizing that her voice had nearly died away and he probably couldn't hear her. Little tremors were running up and down her spine. "I just can't think, Bob. Why Philadelphia? And why next week? I don't think I can get ready next week, Bob."

"Come to meet me in Portland tomorrow morning. I'll leave my car and fly. I've got to see you."

"That's nice, Bob. We missed you Christmas," she said.

"You asked about Philadelphia. Well, Philadelphia's pretty close to Pittsburgh, but a little nicer for a honeymoon."

"I heard about the Pirates, Bob."

"Well, I've signed with them, Honey. Closed the deal yesterday. I've been pretty darned busy, and I did try to call you."

"Yes, Aunt Ellen said you had. Did you forget I was home?"

"Guess I celebrated a little too much. But don't hold it against me. We won a pretty hard game."

"I watched you play over TV. I saw you catch that pass."

"Good girl! I'll make a ball player's wife out of you after all. Better call your Aunt Ellen and tell her to hunt someone to take your place. She can send your things to you."

"Oh!" she gulped.

Her mind whirling, she thought, I can't go away from the shop right now. I can't marry Bob next week. "There's some unfinished business in San Francisco," she said.

"What, Tracy? I just can't hear you. Bad connection, I suppose."

"Oh, Bob, it's not altogether that. I just can't think because you took me so by surprise. I have to have more time; it wouldn't be fair to leave without notice."

"No one's indispensable, you know. I'll bet they can get someone else to take your place."

"Bob, instead of your coming right up here, why don't you wait for me to come down? I had planned on coming tomorrow. They are expecting me."

"They can just un-expect you then. You won't need the job any longer, Honey. Why, you should hear what I'll be getting next season. We'll have a little caviar now and then."

His idea of being a wealthy plutocrat! he'd often said.

"Bob, I just can't think right now. I'll call you back in half an hour. What number shall I call?"

"But I was just ready to leave the apartment. Oh, well, I can wait. I don't see why you can't make up your mind, though."

As she replaced the receiver, Tracy shivered. Make up her mind in five minutes about marrying next week? Why did that seem a light decision to Bob? It would affect so many people. A quick succession of faces flitted through her mind. The parade started with Miles Stewart and ended with Miles Stewart.

20

AVOIDING the two girls and her brother, she went directly to her room for privacy and a chance to think. She couldn't discuss her problem with anyone else. This had to be her own decision. If she talked it over with her mother, she might be influenced by something her mother said. This is something I have to live with all the days of my life, she told herself.

Marriage is forever.

Tracy sat beside her window for a long time. She still had four minutes to go when she went to the small den upstairs and placed her call.

Bob was impatient. She could tell that from the first sound of his voice.

"Bob, I'm terribly sorry, but I just can't run away and leave things unfinished. I have to return to San Francisco tomorrow as I promised."

"You mean you think more of that

stupid job than you do of me?" Amazement made his voice sharp.

She spoke very gently. "Of course not Bob. But there are certain things I have to do."

"Name two," he demanded.

She laughed lightly. "Come now, Bob. It must have occurred to you that a girl needs a little time. You had never even told me about the Pirates wanting you."

"You've been pretty busy, Tracy. I've tried once or twice to talk to you, but you didn't seem very interested."

"You've never mentioned the Pirates to me, Bob," she said spiritedly. "It would mean we'd live in the East, wouldn't it?"

"Well, partly, of course. Part of the time I'd be in training, too. You could always go along with me. Lots of the wives do."

"Bob, I just don't think I could get ready for a wedding by next week, to be honest."

"It doesn't have to be a big, fancy wedding with all the trimmings."

"I know, but I did promise my parents that we'd have a church wedding, and they're not really something you whip up at a moment's notice. There are the announcements—the invitations, rather—and—" She broke off.

"Oh, for Pete's sake! Don't tell me you'd have to have all the parties and everything else to go with them."

By the conclusion of the call they were both unhappy, but Bob had promised to meet her plane.

When it landed the next day, there was a call for her as she went into the terminal building. It was a message that Bob had been unavoidably detained by business and suggested that she take a taxi home.

She was just getting ready to pick up her luggage at the counter when Miles came quickly forward. "Gee! I had a time parking in all the rush. Kennedy kept me at the shop too long. I meant to be here when your plane landed."

Tracy beamed at him. He caught up her hands. "You didn't think I'd let you take a cab, did you?" He turned to the attendant. "Hold these a bit longer, will you? We need to get some lunch."

Without asking, he tucked her hand into his arm and they went upstairs to the Pancake Palace. They found a small table, and were soon discussing all the events which had happened since they'd last seen each other.

It makes it very difficult, seeing Miles so soon after being asked to marry Bob next week. But of course that's what made the decision so hard, she told herself honestly.

Only her mother knew of the problem; she had not confided in the others. But she knew her mother would have a conclave with her father when he came home from work that night.

Her mother's only words had been, "I think you did the right thing in taking a little longer."

Miles took her home a little later, and she thanked him again for meeting her. He had not attempted to kiss her, and she was grateful to him for that.

Bob called her about eight o'clock. "Look, Tracy, I meant to meet you, and then, too, I thought we'd go out tonight, but something's come up. Pretty important, too, involving my contract termination on this team. You understand, don't you?"

"Certainly, Bob." A little inner sigh

welled up. After all, it gave her a few more hours' relief from seeing him and having to go through another serious discussion about why she must have longer than a week's notice to get ready to marry him.

She came down for a chat with her Aunt Ellen about nine o'clock.

"I'm glad you came, dear, for I was going to your room presently. Come on over by the fire, and I'll have Mattie bring in some tea. You look a little more rested, but you still could do with another week, I think."

"I'm fine. I needed to get back, Auntie Ellen."

They discussed the holiday and the visit with her family. Tracy had the feeling that her aunt had something to tell her about the shop, and finally asked her if she had any information.

"Yes. I hated to tell you about it, but I presume you should know. I made out a list of valuable books that I thought might have been sold by now, and among them was the *Secret Diary of A Southern General*. Mr. Kennedy says it has been lost. It was worth about two thousand dollars."

"But I saw that very book not too long ago," Tracy said in dismay. "I had no idea it was that valuable."

"You saw it?" asked Ellen eagerly.

"Yes. First in the anteroom, then later down in the vaults." She caught her lip. She hadn't planned to let her aunt know that she had secretly gone to the vaults.

Her aunt was telling her about the sudden rise in the value of the book. "It's one of those sudden things that are always happening. It's on a new listing as one of the most valuable books published in that century. I found it myself in the new catalogue."

"Were all the other books sold?" Tracy referred to the list Ellen and her attorney had discussed with Kennedy.

"Either sold, or accounted for. Mr. Kennedy has asked to buy the shop, but I'm not at all happy at the thought of selling. I've told him so before."

"If there's so little profit to be had, it seems strange that he should be so insistent about buying."

"I'm holding off the answer until the first of April."

"Good. That should give you some time to consider."

Time to consider, *time to consider*. If she stayed on until April, it would give *her* time to consider. But then Bob would want her to marry him before the beginning of the baseball season. Soon she excused herself and went up to bed.

The last thing she thought of before dropping off to sleep was that she would take the earliest possible opportunity to go to the vault again.

The chance did not come until two days later, although she rose betimes her first day back and went to the shop early. Kennedy was already there. He greeted her as though it were any ordinary day. She looked about the shop and saw that all of the Christmas decorations had been taken down and either burned or put away for next year.

She was busy all day long, not going out for coffee either in the morning or the afternoon. She saw Iris at lunch, and they spent just a few minutes looking in at shop windows before returning to their work. Knowing that Bob was coming out to her aunt's for dinner, she purposely avoided giving Miles the chance to ask her for a date.

"Are you avoiding me?" grinned Miles. "Or did you know that I've been following you, ma'am?"

"I thought I was being followed, Officer!" she said.

"I take it that Bob's back and you're going out with him?"

She was honest with him. "He's coming out to dinner."

"I read the papers, and I see that the Pirates are after him."

She longed to say, "*and they got him*," but it would be announced when the publicity was ready she supposed. As yet, she probably had no right to report on his new job.

"See you tomorrow, then. Save an evening for me soon?"

She nodded. She went home dreading the discussion she knew was impending with Bob. At the last moment she was reprieved again.

"Honey, it's unpardonable, and I hope you'll make my apologies to your aunt, but I can't make it tonight."

"Oh? She'll be disappointed, Bob, but she'll understand. What happened?"

"We didn't get through, and the meeting has to be continued tonight. I wanted to finish up today, but the manager had other things. Sure sorry, but I'll see you without fail tomorrow evening. What say we take your Aunt Ellen out and show the old girl a time? We could bring her home early."

"I'll ask her and tell you later, Bob. Call me after work?"

"Sure thing. Good night, dear."

The next morning Tracy rose earlier than usual and caught an early bus downtown. It was cold and bleak, and she walked briskly to the shop, opening the door with stiffened fingers.

The main salesroom was almost dark. She crossed the floor without turning on the lights and, going directly to the office, was able to get the keys to the vault. She was exultant, for she hadn't thought they'd be left on the board.

Still turning on no lights, she groped her way down the narrow winding stairs toward the vault. Taking a flashlight from her tote bag, she turned on the light and placed the key in the big steel doors. They swung open easily.

Before stepping inside, she paused to listen carefully. There was not a sound upstairs. She glanced at her watch. It was only seven-forty-five.

She had been unconsciously checking on Mr. Kennedy's arrival time the last two weeks before Christmas. Allowing for the late hours they had all been working during the holiday rush, and for the half-hour leeway he now gave himself before opening time, she still had quite a few minutes. Leaving the outer doors open, she opened the last of the steel doors. Here at last, in the quiet, dim interior, she turned on the lights and closed the inner door. There was no air and the place was warm, and there was a faint musty smell which she always associated with old books in closed rooms.

Suddenly she realized that for once the safe was open. The door stood barely ajar, and she didn't notice it until she was almost touching it. Pointing her flashlight to the interior, she gasped in surprise. There was the very book her aunt had mentioned the night of her arrival.

Supposedly lost, what was it doing here in the vault? In the safe, rather? Was it possible that it had been located and put here for safekeeping? If so, why hadn't Kennedy called her aunt at once?

A small brown leather book lay near it. Picking it up and reading it, Tracy saw that it contained a list of titles which she knew to be rare. There were a few checks in the margin. She counted them, for she could tell they indicated sales. *The Secret Diary* was checked, she noted. And the sum next to it was three thousand, instead of the two her aunt had thought it worth. "To Ludgate of London."

To Ludgate of London! If it were sold, why hadn't it been mailed to them?

Tracy suddenly stood upright. She had heard a noise outside the door. Panicky, she looked for a place to hide.

There was nowhere to hide, she thought as she flicked off her flashlight. She heard keys in the lock. Shaking violently, she realized that she had left the outer doors open, so whoever it was would know that someone was in the vault.

The inner door was jerked open, and then the overhead light flashed on.

Kennedy stood in the doorway, holding a gun. He fired, but the bullet went wild. "Miss Allen!" he shouted. Lowering the gun, he just stood staring at her.

"What are you doing down here?" He crossed the room.

She tried to answer, but no words came through her white lips.

"Snooping! You've snooped before. What were you expecting to find?"

"What is there to find, Mr. Kennedy?"

He turned and strode swiftly back to the door. "I'll give you time to think that out. You'll find it a little cold, a little damp down here. The oxygen will give out, too, I'm told."

Before her startled eyes, he turned off the lights, swung the inner door closed, locked it, and then barred it from the outside. She heard the clang of the big outer steel doors, and then there was silence. For a moment she was too stunned to think. Would he just leave her in here? But of course Miles would ask about her, would even call her aunt to inquire if she were sick. But Kennedy could say she'd called him. She could stay closed up in there all day. Her aunt would call, but suppose no one was there to answer the telephone? A dozen quick thoughts flashed through her mind, and when she lighted her way to turn on the lights again, Tracy found she could barely move.

But Kennedy had thought of everything, she thought morosely, even turning the lights off at the switch outside!

There was a ladder, a small stool. At least she could sit down. What would Kennedy do with her? He couldn't afford just to turn her loose, of course. She began to shake when the full impact of her predicament struck her.

Suddenly she straightened. There was the sound of scuffling, the sound of someone or something hitting the outer doors. After a moment, silence; then she heard the key in the outer door, and in a moment the inner door.

It was pushed open by a disheveled Miles Stewart. His lip was bleeding, his eye was cut, and a lump was swelling on his chin. He muttered, "Tracy! Oh, Tracy!"

She felt his hard arms around her, lifting her up and sheltering her. "Are you all right, darling?"

She gasped out feebly, "Miles! Not so tightly! I'm all right!"

"I almost killed Kennedy!" He set her down, and she touched his chin. "Miles! Oh, Miles, I'm sorry."

"It'll be all right. Better go up and call the police."

"Yes, dear." She moved toward the door.

"Hey, wait!" Miles reached her and, putting his arm about her, said, "Say that again, please."

"What?"

"That word. 'Dear,' it sounded like."

"Oh, that word? Dear Miles!" Reaching on her tiptoes, she placed a kiss on his chin before he caught her and kissed her with the side of his lips which were not bleeding.

Now everything will be all right, Tracy thought as she hurried up the narrow steps. Her answer to Bob was ready, and the problems her aunt had known at the shop were about to be solved. She dialed Bob, realizing that she could never have married him. Never, once she had met Miles.

GUIDE
TO THE COLOUR CODING
OF
ULVERSCROFT BOOKS

Many of our readers have written to us expressing their appreciation for the way in which our colour coding has assisted them in selecting the Ulverscroft books of their choice. To remind everyone of our colour coding— this is as follows:

BLACK COVERS
Mysteries

★

BLUE COVERS
Romances

★

RED COVERS
Adventure Suspense and General Fiction

★

ORANGE COVERS
Westerns

★

GREEN COVERS
Non-Fiction

ROMANCE TITLES
in the
Ulverscroft Large Print Series

THE SHADOWS
OF THE CROWN TITLES
in the
Ulverscroft Large Print Series

The Tudor Rose   *Margaret Campbell Barnes*
Brief Gaudy Hour *Margaret Campbell Barnes*
Mistress Jane Seymour   *Frances B. Clark*
My Lady of Cleves
                    Margaret Campbell Barnes
Katheryn The Wanton Queen
                              Maureen Peters
The Sixth Wife   *Jean Plaidy*
The Last Tudor King   *Hester Chapman*
Young Bess   *Margaret Irwin*
Lady Jane Grey   *Hester Chapman*
Elizabeth, Captive Princess   *Margaret Irwin*
Elizabeth and The Prince of Spain
                            Margaret Irwin
Gay Lord Robert   *Jean Plaidy*
Here Was A Man   *Norah Lofts*
Mary Queen of Scotland:
The Triumphant Year   *Jean Plaidy*
The Captive Queen of Scots   *Jean Plaidy*
The Murder in the Tower   *Jean Plaidy*
The Young and Lonely King   *Jane Lane*
King's Adversary   *Monica Beardsworth*
A Call of Trumpets   *Jane Lane*

FICTION TITLES
in the
Ulverscroft Large Print Series

The Onedin Line: The High Seas
                                Cyril Abraham

The Onedin Line: The Iron Ships
                                Cyril Abraham

The Onedin Line: The Shipmaster
                                Cyril Abraham

The Onedin Line: The Trade Winds
                                Cyril Abraham

The Enemy	*Desmond Bagley*
Flyaway	*Desmond Bagley*
The Master Idol	*Anthony Burton*
The Navigators	*Anthony Burton*
A Place to Stand	*Anthony Burton*
The Doomsday Carrier	*Victor Canning*
The Cinder Path	*Catherine Cookson*
The Girl	*Catherine Cookson*
The Invisible Cord	*Catherine Cookson*
Life and Mary Ann	*Catherine Cookson*
Maggie Rowan	*Catherine Cookson*
Marriage and Mary Ann	*Catherine Cookson*
Mary Ann's Angels	*Catherine Cookson*
All Over the Town	*R. F. Delderfield*
Jamaica Inn	*Daphne du Maurier*
My Cousin Rachel	*Daphne du Maurier*

NON-FICTION TITLES
in the
Ulverscroft Large Print Series

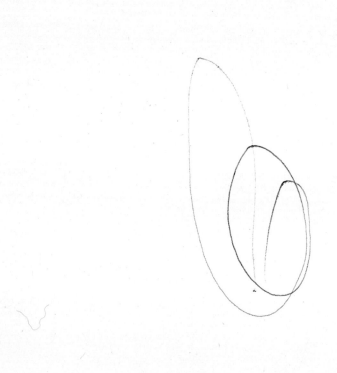